THE METAVERSE

Isaac Ekow Anyidoho
THE METAVERSE

Published by Spines
ISBN: 979-8-89569-314-8

THE METAVERSE

Step into the void

Isaac Ekow Anyidoho

Contents

ABOUT THE BOOK vii

TERMS ix

THE ASSEMBLY 1

THE CONTACT 7

FILL THE VOID 16

TERMINALS 30

THE SHY HILLS 45

ROYAL HABITS 59

FISH BONE 87

THE SAKURA 112

TABLE OF MEN 132

ABOUT THE BOOK

In the beginning of the Metaverse was the Meta; where all were given an equal life opportunity to dream a dream and to also explore where ever one wishes to explore with a virtual dreaming device.

But never did the residents of the Metaverse know that; the very spirit and attitude that possess you during the physical world is the same spirit and attitude that will possess you during the Metaverse until it happened...... And John Cool was right, for what they cooked in their minds was the very aroma that followed them all day long. And, at a place where the act of believing in God is absent, I just can't say may God help us. For who is God to be considered in the affairs of the Metaverse!!

The Youngins were lost yet never trusting the old guys for direction as they say, "To every front door is another back door."

TERMS

TERM	MEANING
Meta-Quart	Supremacy
Meta-terra	Power
Meta-Zone	Authority
Meta-light	Intelligence
Meta-Das	1st Degree level
Meta-dash	2nd Degree level
Meta-Qark	3rd Degree level
Meta-cedi	Currency (1MC= 15.7 USD)
Meta-cat	Negative acts (theft, cheating, etc.)
Meta-craft	Evil acts (bullying, insults, etc.)
Meta-sphere or Metaverse	Meta-world
Metadata	Packet of Information (200 meta-bytes of meta-data per 2 second.)
Metapol	Police Officer (on the Meta)
Meta-card	A microchip with financial Infor.)
Meta-Prizzin	Prison or jail
Meta-Blaqq	Blacklist platform
Meta-court	Law court
Youngins	Youths or Young Adults
VIPS	Virtual Intersection Protons Screen

THE ASSEMBLY

The young lanky tall Sub-Saharan dark man whose smooth, naked, and hairless arms were as empty as the vast Sahara Desert without trees arrived at Southampton Street; His hairless face was dried up even after much strength exerted on pulling his baggage due to the cold air streaming around the area, in an attempt of crossing the street he was almost hit by a passing car due to the left-hand drive system compared to where he comes from but found himself at the other side of the road and began to catch his breath.

Well across the NW21 street, he heads toward a private health facility reserved for old and mentally unstable people in their seventies and reports to the officer in charge and presents his credentials and also a black and white letter stating his appointment to work as a male Health Assistant. He sat down without being asked to and asked for water which he did not get only for the letter to be taken away and into the next room where a phone call was made and a confirmation was made to his claims. Taken to the second floor of the building by Nancy, he was greeted by a small room with no bed, chair, or table the last time it received a human occupant was about twenty-eight months back, the small room was cold, dark and stuffy to the smell with a small green light bulb at the side of the window. Nancy smiled and added have a nice stay, and see you tomorrow at six o'clock prompt to meet other working staff in here. Without dusting about and cleaning, he lay his old cloth on the floor and lay down thinking of all the ordeals he went into before reaching Britain in person, the cost, the delay, and the discouragement from friends and family whom he thought meant well for his life but did not. In the partly dark room whose washroom he is yet to check if it's in good order, he suddenly felt an insect moving across his left exposed leg upon checking was one of the well-known brown insects called cockroach which is picked battled with and won in less than forty-five seconds using his bear left hand to do the strike. With tissue wiped his palm and never cared about the washroom.

The cold and dark night compared to an African standard airflow was different and sudden to his lanky human frame but what else matters, work is what brought him across the mountains and at his own will and choice. He lay there far asleep, sleeping like a sudden fallen tree which is never getting up on its feet as the crawling insects zips around him with others climbing his human body like a mountaineer crossing the steep side of the Alps with ropes.

Once in a while the partly dead human body moves and shifts on his made-shift mat making the insects scatter and wonder what is happening to their path. He woke up in the dead of the night and turned the light on only to see how the hundreds of insects all over his body and almost making him a zoo and began to kill them starting with shaking his clothes. He looked for water which was half half-empty water bottle helped him out after looking for the washroom. Locating the small room serving as toilet and bathroom, he turned on the light only to be greeted with a foul smell and cockroaches playing all over the room as if in a sports arena; with a shock and a bit of surprise, he did his back side of his business and closed the door hard not caring about waking the others along the floor. Checking the time, it was one and a half hours to the medical reporting time, and did not sleep again only to do some checks and read his map about the town in which he now finds himself.

The Southampton township on the map looks vast compared to what he knows from Africa and even begins to wonder if it's that big then how bigger will London be in reality? From the Open market to the Central Health facility, the Police Department and the Fire Engine Department which are just two hundred meters away from each other are painted almost with the same color looking like twins in their morning colorful dress for a school party. Then comes a large and spacious building where some section of worshipers from the Christian faith meet labeled Church of England followed by the medium side Baptist church. There was a Mosque too at the far end of the long street as if placed there to prevent an unknown hostility among the growing youth of the area as the only television studio sits ninety degrees from the Police Department. The Taxi stops are dotted along only Brood Street and about two hundred meters interval with the bus station very close to the rial terminal which leads to London and other notable city centers of the country. London, Leeds, and Glasgow are the very common names he can see across the pocket map in his hands. With courage and hope went into the washroom again and turned the tap on, began to clean and wash his face, and cleaned himself up a bit. With his teeth washed, cleaned his black footwear with a tissue and pulled out a file containing some documents only to ready himself for the meeting downstairs.

Meanwhile, ten other health service workers had already arrived at the main office as news began to filter in that; new staff had reported and were ready to work. With those gathered in there were five registered Nurses, two assistant Nurses, a degree Nurse, a Health Coordinator, Facility Keeper. And then suddenly, he appeared and smiled at them only to see two other African complexion people but not Africans but are British by nationality. The Health Co-Ordinator acting as manager welcomed him and introduced him to the other working staff and that was all.

In the common silent room despite being filled with people who need care and special attention, the well-lite and warm room qualified to be called a hall, then if so; the warm Hall had twelve special people all seated in their chairs calmly, cleaned, and clothed as they silently filter the streaming morning new around the country on Channel five television transmitting from London. In the best of their silence, each person glued himself or herself in the soft armchair distance from the other by one and a half meters as they waited for further instructions from their caregivers. Out of the twelve were four old women Hannah once a nurse, Margaret a retired medical doctor, Tracy a broadcaster and Mary who is an old Indian merchant in fact; a trader in Asian perfumery and carpets who lost all her family in a single day due to a domestic fire accident starting from the kitchen area. All senior citizens are above the age of sixty-five years and a combined age of eight hundred of ninety-two years old which is becoming a problem to them with several among them not able to walk more than ten meters without assistance from a nurse or walking stick. The old men are all calm, and ready and also are the very ones who aim at and always do according to what their caregivers say; they are the very end of the word of order or "do before complain". After Frank Kofi Settor was introduced to them as Frank; one of the new Nursing assistants who will serve them with patience and kindness, all care receivers smiled, with some waving their partly weak hands as seated and about one centimeter from the arms of their chairs.

Given just two hours to report for full duty when the handy-woman arrived, Franky took her up and helped her with the door to repair all broken locks and also work on the leaking sink as well as service the assigned furniture to be pulled out from the next empty room. Upon showing up, he looked at the caregiver feeding Mary one of the most unstable old women around with her morning meals before her medications which is a total of six emotion and mental stability tablets as directed by the primary physician from the general hospital. Franky reached out to Tracy and began to feed her too. From one person to the other, the second morning ritual feeding was done after bathing and right after that, the big screen television was turned on making all watch a bit of entertainment to kick start the day. At times the caregivers sing or have set up their sort of musical team where they sing with them for close to two hours and it's one of the acts where they are also asked to do likewise; singing along to popular music and anthems during their hay days in London, Paris, and Berlin just to mention a few. By afternoon, all were glued to the twelve new headsets donated by Vodaphone during their thirstiest anniversary of operation to the care home for them to know what is new and here we go.

With the headsets mounted for each person, only God knows what each person dives into and due to their condition, not much is discussed after. The donation by Vodaphone has been able to make each care receiver in the facility own two worlds being; here which is the Universe and there which is the Metaverse. With their ups and downs; they now walk on the corridors of the Multiverse.

THE CONTACT

You see, this place called the universe for which nothing is free has its own rules and regulations which some say is fair but from a common viewpoint has never been fair since the early hours of creation.

1. There is no free lunch no matter the location.
2. Never take what is not yours but that does not apply to the politician.
3. Mind your own business if you value your life, drug traffickers say.
4. Pay your taxes which is a casual joke to some people in society.
5. Money Makes the World Go Round is another old song sung at night.
6. Observers are worried, is the rich list slogan of the year.
7. Tell me who is God and I will show you the wickedness of this world.

8. Call the Police and I will call the lawmaker.
9. Racism is the next world order.
10. Cash is the new anthem of this world.

In this part of the universe called Earth, not everybody can have a dream and even so, those who dream a dream require a level of understanding, awareness, and courage to make things happen but that may not be so in the metaverse. In the metaverse, anybody can have a dream, a sort of electronic dream that never expires and may never harm the lives on whom those dreams are placed. Then the face plate, it's a well-crafted plastic setup filled with hundreds of tiny electronic sensors, capacitors, transistors, and semiconductors to transform and make electronic imaging and vision casting. After just one hour of charging, the face plate is placed well across the front of the human head and covers both eyes like the act of wearing sunglasses only to be fastened at the back of the head to hold the sleek gadget into place and once turn on, makes the user fall into an electronic trance and to behold what lies within the meta. There are laws and despite those laws, the **Meta-terra** which is the power of the metaverse can be challenged with a level of clear understanding called **Meta-light**.

Well, look there; he who sits there is Mr. Alex James Hyde a retired civil servant who once worked with the London water and sewage company, a father of four clearer boys; well now a man who works in the city of London with different banks and as at now does not know where their father lives. During his mid-fifties in age, he was suddenly taken ill and hospitalized for close to six months only to be diagnosed as a dementia patient and with slight nervous challenge in the head as brain cells quakes like a sparking electric current hence called in for early retirement. A. J. Hyde was born in the early summer morning of 1965 in Leeds to a locksmith father whose skill set serviced the locks and doors of a local Lord and the town for close to thirty-seven years and a mother who sold smoked fish at the local market nearby. During his boyhood, he worn the affection of the Lord whom his father worked for only to be given a scholarship to study in York with all expenses paid for after graduation in chemistry accepted a post as a water quality officer with the London water and sewage company where he met the good, the bad and not all that ugly kind of people who should have been sent to the Tower of London for a royal execution but then blending in and escape is part of their skill set in life.

During a duty call, he once saw a floating human hand floating at the surface of the raw water intake tank and wondered what was happening. Am I dreaming or awake? He said to himself after tapping his cheeks twice. Whose hand is this? Is anybody missing a hand which must be always part of himself or herself huh? And who is cooking people's hands for supper? With all these questions, the loudest answer he got was silence and that was it. Alex books a report, called in the London Police and that was that the problem was never solved. And he was never accused too of any wrongdoing as a chemist working the waters for use in most homes in and around the city of London. He stands at five and half feet tall and is the second tallest among his siblings yet very calm and worries much about his future as if told that all will crumple upon him and a lover of money as he thinks money can solve all problems or money can make any problem go away, as such he is quick to be led into any kind of deal with hopes and promises of making huge cash at the end of the day and it's on this note that he came across James Small, a second term member of the House of Commons in London.

You have entered another regional area... was the very next word that the metaverse announced. A cold, wide, and white landscape with large animal dominance like polar bears, Seawolf, penguins, and other animals which the recent world has lost touch with in fact sparse or almost empty human interference or dominance. A grey and tall woman soon surfaced and asked what is wanted in a strange language if not Russian then I know not. Well, he received another three hundred terabytes of meta-data in just under three seconds only to understand what the woman is saying and his response will be understood in Russian too. The white woman answered which made her stop talking, freeze up, and ask again which era are you coming from huh? My name is Rexford Stone born in a part of the Universe called Earth and in a local continental area called England, does that ring a bell to you? But then where is this place, who owns and controls it and where do you people get your food? Ohhh, you are from the world ahead in time, and am told that you people act silly towards another based on skin color, wayward towards your elderly and parents, and full of hate. Is that the case? Maravich said to Rexford...Well, I conclude and will not try to convince either that that is not the case... the world I was born into was different and currently, it has changed again which is not my doing or my singular fault; well hope I have answered that question well, he said with a soft smile. We are the people of Russ who speak the Russian language and own this place, don't worry about where and how we get our food for it's not to be told to strangers like you man.

The woman vanished only for a young male to surface asking where is your weapon and how did you get there. The young male pulled his sword and in a stepwise act began to walk towards Rexford who smiled thinking to calm him down the man was determined and getting angry by the second but then two men about six feet tall willing two black revolving guns to their side and a hand cop each with enough meta-Zone seized him and took him away. The meta-sphere also known as the Metaverse has its own rules and regulations and on top of those rules are degrees of operation; they wore a blue-black uniform with a pair of boots to march, guns to their side either male or female, a metallic chain to grip and a set of communicating device which is well connected to their meta-data and meta-light gaining and giving information to their co-workers and intelligent officers and enforcers to work well. They are a set of Metapol about one hundred and twenty million strong, armed, and with fifty thousand top officers giving orders to enforce the rules and regulations of that world.

With the Metapol handling the situation, Rexford took a sign of relief, and turned around only to appear in Wales; that old and silent village countryside controlled by the government of Britain. Rexford was very surprised, happy to see the land of his birth hundreds of years back and comparing it to what it now looks and was like, oh what a big village... born in nineteen forty-six, just a year after that great old war; he was the very perfect gift from God the ruler of the Spirit-verse Mr. and Mrs. Stone who have been childless after twelve faithful years of marriage which both sides of their families did not agree to and denial them of any blessings from day one of their union. They lack accommodation, food, farmland, and any sort of property that will make raising a family a bit easier. The joy, gladness, and thankfulness of having a child was what occupied their minds much so that, they sold their only working wagon to buy the three sheep to start a farm on a rented farmland belonging to a local Lord called Lord Ransford Cotton. After his secondary education at Oxford minor, he was lucky to be accepted into the local police unit where he worked for six years after saving enough to attend the London School of Economics and today, he is a retired banker.

The sudden shaking of his hand as his body resides in the chair of this mortal gave the health keeps an indication that he needs help and as soon as the electronic gadget was removed, he was served with water and looked at the nurse blinking his eyes in appreciation. Looking at the nurse like a kid, the gadget was placed again and this time it was a different experience....

"You see in the Metaverse, what you imagine is what you see, and what you see is what you will get and eventually where you will be" ... that is, it's yours to choose the type of meta-light you deserve as a being, it's all about choices.

The much older pair Mary and Tracy; traveled to Tasmania with a twinkle of an eye blink as they showed up in a medium-sized shopping mall owned by a group called Load-stone Incorporation which has been in existence or opera-tion for close to ten years now. And girls will always be girls... they brushed off the line-up set of gym tools only to arrive at the lady bag collection, seeing, pointing, and collecting what their money can buy. With their Meta-cards the shopping spree began, Mary picked up two black hand-bags from Luis Vuitton and a purse from Adidas only to add

I need more... as Tracy walked to the lane of hanging ladies' cotton woven scarfs and some of the colors were black, red, white, light brown, coffee brown, dark coal black, sea blue, off-white and many others which can dazzle a woman to say yes without knowing. The Meta-card is just like an ATM card housing the personal information of the holder from health records, financial account records, Family History records, race, every geographical spot you have ever visited on earth, social information including nutritional needs, basic events attended, and even sexual orientation and also security clearance information if even you are a Royal on earth. These and many other information are stored on the meta-card except religious affiliation as technology and science rule the metaverse. With one meta-cedi being equal to fifteen-point seven United States dollars, the grown-up girls were killing it in Tasmania.

Rexford; after wondering through the long line of shops on Wall Street was fed-up and wanting a new experience closed his eyes as if wanting to pray which the last time, he ever did that was during his secondary school days; in fact, the last Tuesday before their last examination where all were assembled to say a prayer in the dining hall. With that short blink, he opened his eyes only to see himself in a typical Turkish massage café called Hammam. He changed his cloths leaving a small short pants and entered the steam room, where the in initial heat filling the room nearly made him run off but stay as after a short ten-minute warm-up, he was then introduced to a cool and chilled water bath which made the difference to be clear. A huge tall masculine man whose arms are filled with enough human hair almost looks like the Bush man's tall graces of South Africa where big cats hide to make a kill. He lay prostrate on to the white marble floor where the man after pouring some brown creams began to scrub him up with a soft woven locally prepared cleaning item as the foaming nature tears his eyes. Later a sweet smell of nectar was added as enough water was used to wash him up.

Finally; he was wiped dry, oiled with some aromatic oils, and cooled down with a soft drink. The Turkish massage dating back to the era before the Romans has kept it standard and purpose such that even other nations yearn for it to be practiced in their territories, as its good for soldiers returning from war.

With the renowned strength of a twenty-one-year-old man, he rushed into a Spanish casino on the street of New York called The Dot, as if wanting to explore all other aspects of life which he never did during his active years. He showed up around a table with other five sets of men each purchasing eight hundred thousand casino chips each amounting to three hundred thousand meta-cedi; each guarded his chips before him as if it were the straw of their life. Hey, where are you all from, Rexford said after picking up his gaming chips... come on dude are you ready to play or not? Grab a seat and let the game roll another fanny face-looking man said making the others smile. With all set, the double dice were cast as they rolled on the table with the number wheel turning as each player aimed at hoping his side of the number worked. With ten minutes to the top of the hour, the nurse on duty began tapping all one after the other at their shoulder making them aware it was time to report home from wherever they were; from Rexford, Mary, Tracy, and others. The electronic gadgets were removed for them to eat, and take their medications and all were happy if not shown by the smile, then by blinking their eyes as they looked at their caregiver's face.

A.J. Hyde was the very last person for his gadget to be removed, but guess what? He run into his old wife the last time they separated was about twenty-five years ago and once they had no child, both parties have never attempted contacting the other; in a Japanese art store on the busy streets of Osaka, they looked eyes for the first time and as two old fire woods, the chemistry was right as from story-lines, none of them know what caused their breakup, as childlessness is a secondary matter. Hello, Rexford said as the best of feminine soft tone hello my man, where have you been all these years? He stretched out his hand for a hand-shake but the handshake was denied as her girlfriends looked on.

With the gadget removed and in a state of not able to say what is expected due to his clinical conditions, tears began to stream down his wrinkled cheeks as if told that all was lost and the health care providers could not decide what took place apart from himself. The meta-light can't be trans-ferred without being in the metaverse.

FILL THE VOID

The metaverse is but a virtual world built not for the rich and poor, not for the weak and lowly, and never meant to be a place for racism, corruption, and any religious sects as it has been in the place of the universe called earth but for like minds with the next generation of meta-light.

To enter the void, a well-crafted electronic device called Oculus Quest VR set is placed across the eye to receive vision and sound, again the headset which is popularly called the face plate is like an Android phone strapped to the head to bring vision motion and sound to you in real-time. Meta means more comprehension as the verse stands for a medium which in our case world; the interactions of the Meta are both augmented reality and virtual reality to bring users, sellers, explorers, inventors, academics, and many others together on one platform. In most cases after just one hour of charging using electricity, the face plate is placed well across the front of the human head and covers both sets of eyes like the act of wearing sunglasses only to be fastened at the back of the head to hold the sleek gadget into place and once turn on, you will fall into an electronic trance and to behold what lies within the meta. The meta-terra can support all classes of life from children, youth, parents, grandparents, workers, religious leaders, military heads and officers, job owners, royals, authorities and even commoners and he who enters is promised a meta-light. Again, see the metaverse and the computer age or the internet revolution verse two and you must behold to belong.

Even after the horrific motor accident where he sustained a fractured spina cord, Mr. Jerson Jetson Raymond a chemist sits calmly in his seat well supported with several shock absorbing materials which even so, he can't sit upright for more than one hour. Just ten minutes after feeding, a nurse strapped the face plate across the seeing eyes of J. J. Raymond who is one of a kind among the rest. After his spinal injuries, he also sustained several cuts to his forehead cheeks, and left side of his neck which took seven surgeries to fix that medical problem lasting almost thirty-six months in the Grey Medical hospital in York and to any who suddenly set eye on him and ask what kind of surgery is that? The medical stitches on his forehead which lacked enough human flesh and the side of his cheeks made the whole thing look like cosmetic surgery just gone too far. Well, there he stands, calm and wondering what caused the builder to build such a huge object and also what lies in there. Mr. Raymond receives more than five hundred meta-lights of reasoning power and would get more based on what and where he wishes to be stands silently in the open dry land allowing thousands of dry sandy particles to partly bury his foot, seeing and talking to himself.

Please keep up the pace of walking, request for more meta-light where needed, and don't forget to drink from the bottle strapped by your side as the heat in here can dry you out in minutes, she respectfully added... welcomed by the entrance, the well-crafted building which has stood the test of time is very impressive, huge, strong and wonders who was the very architect who did the draws and how was he schooled? Well, that is if that person was a He... at a four-degree slope of depression, they soon began walking along the well-lite dry corridor with a bit of reduced air supply but breathable till the first empty tomb showed up as Miss Fatimah said once belonged to a Noble stabbed to death by another noble in his sleep. Well, as you can see now his remains have long been taken or stolen by grave looters some centuries back for Black Persian Magic or Charm. The charms and spells written on the walls of the tomb did little to stop those looters who after taking the fine jewels of gold, diamond, and other rubies, were bold to go away with the entire still body. From one point to another, the rubber of those centuries enriched themselves from the sad faith of the occupants, the family, and rubbishing the culture of the people of Egypt.

Meanwhile Mary and Tracy after the short break, began planning a move on their own and when they had their Occulus quest replaced, they paid their way into the ongoing Oxfam Comedy Show in Melbourne, Australia catching up with all the fans that they missed in their adult-hood. With ticket number forty-six and ticket number fifty-eight-A, they walked hurriedly like many others wanting to take their seat ahead of time to see and to be seen. The seating arrangement was such that Mary was at the left hand of the next roll where they could see and touch each other within a hand stretch. There were two female nobles in their prime belonging to the land and people of Thailand dressed in their western dark brown clothes and blending in for the show. With just one royal guard posing like a friend, they rushed in after their electronic tickets paid for by the guard and soon vanished into the sea of people assembled there. The twenty-one thousand seating capacity hall was getting full by the minute as more and more people from distant lands like Africa, Japan, China, Alaska, Texas, Siberia local celebrities, and even two well-known Brazilian businesswomen were all present for the much talk show that year.

A tall lanky Australian man walked onto the stage almost looking like an East African dude who had lost some eating days of his own, six feet tall in his black jeans up and down cloth holding the microphone and yelling... Are you ready!!!!! ... how is the going people, tell me... and even as he spoke, a good young and sleek beautiful young lady also emerged from the back who joined him only to ask, can you feel me!!! The crowd went wild after seeing her good looks in the all-white short skirt with a short and hanging top cloth exposing her nipple, a kind of Las Vegas showgirl in Australia.

To remove hate which sometimes leads to racism, hurt, and offense for a lack of better use of words, the Meta-Quart through the meta-zone assigned all seated there a higher degree of tolerance and understanding which in this case can be referred to as Comedy meta-light as all were on the same level and dimension of state to make merry and to have fun.

Well... well... well, when Tony Wood a retired bank rubber having robbed close to twenty-eight banks in his active duty, cashing three hundred and twenty million dollars with his men who are all feared dead and gone and never caught by any law institution till now entered the meta; guess what he saw? Alfred Fox, one of the fastest drivers he has ever worked with, and Peter Lobster a seasoned route planner, stood silently with their hands folded to their chests as if they knew he was coming. With about two hundred meta-data acts on and a huge meta-light of understanding on what to do and what not to do, he walked towards his friends perhaps for old time's sake, and shook hands with them as the Metapol in their fast-flying cars passed by. They crossed the busy road only to sit down on the side chair and began to pick up from where they left off some sixteen years back.

In the avatar of their full self, the three men walking in the city of Stockholm envisioned London, and behold they were there, standing at the Piccadilly station and they smiled. Walking side by side in the mild afternoon sunshine of London, they walked towards the Llyod Merchant Bank which they had robbed before about sixteen years back and entered as the bank's welcome sign greeted them with good hopes of doing good business. Peter and Alfred sat allowing Tony to step forward and to do the talking as if wanting to use their services to pay a client in India to supply him tea leaves that same week. As long as the tall goes on with the front desk or the relationship banker, the two seated were taking notes of positions, blind sports, electronic entry and exit systems in place, the security team on standby, and even who among them is the bank manager and bank accountant. Again, Peter went further writing on a small piece of paper as if writing the numbers of electronic exchange rates being displayed on the walls but that is not so at all, he was keeping notes of the flow of people entering and leaving the banking hall to see if it's a well-used or crowded location being that more money is stored there and such a high volume of people also means they can muddy the waters for their swift escape strategy.

Tony Wood who lost his balance in a shopping mall when climbing one of their stairs and broke his neck was able to sue the mall operators for close to eighty million dollars for negligence and poor floor planning as he spent close to thirteen months at the hospital after two successive surgeries on his neck and with that was taken back and retired under a smooth work out plan after losing about sixty percent of his memory, now can talk well and can't remember where he even stays and comes from; the London authorities assigned him a Care Home and caregivers and truly, no one know who he was and what he has done to the city of London and the entire nation. As for Peter, he locked horns with the authorities and got shot in his head and that was that... Alfred on the other hand picked a fight in a club and was stub by a gang of guys about sixteen times to his chest only to die after the ambulance arrived to pick him up from the hospital he was also never discovered as a robber belonging to the group called "TM" or Team Move.

In as much as the metaverse has a metapol there has never been any time where a crime of any foul play has been committed or left uninvestigated as every meta-light is calibrated, identified, and electronically circumvented. Crime in here is even noticed and picked upon in seconds of their committing without calling the Metapol for help. Just last time Metapol was able to detect a syndicate where a bank staff was aiding two Italian-trained computer system engineers to rub an innocent bank which is just two years into its operation to a sum close to ten million meta-cedi; then they showed up and arrested the Potter Bank staff and the two yet to be robbers stationed about two electronic miles away from the bank only to send to the Meta-zone for action.

That black and short King defended and protected the interest of his people so much and so well that; even the British would dare not pick any of his tribal men or women without informing him through his subjects and in a way the British conformed with some of his rules if not all. The short King subjects may be a threat to other rival chiefdoms and Kingdoms of the forest and other coastal areas and the British knew that too. Should you see any slave coming from the King of Kumasi called Ashanti King among the other slaves means such a person is a nuisance to his or her community and must be sold off.

With just one and a half meta-cedi each, these people sitting well in their seats have been able to tour distant lands, feel the place, ask questions, and do just right.

There; there he sits, calm and well composed once seasoned law enforces chasing after road traffic crimes and other getaways on the twenty-two-freeway connecting northeast to the southwest of the city. Despite being medically sick with a mild motion state, he surfaced in the sideline jungle of East Malaysia which is well known as the Borneo rain forest where it rains almost every day of the week. Well surprised at how able he has become and the growing ability he is gaining, he stopped and looked around only for a grey and able man to walk towards him and introduce himself. Muktuk Aziza a Malay Islam announced his presence with two other aids armed with rifles and showed him the cross-section of the forest cover which is over eighty-six kilometers square and about twelve billion trees whose combined ages will be a million plus-plus years old. Mr. John Iris Rawlings smiled when he was given the sharp forest cutlass only to follow them like a sheep being led to a slaughterhouse without a word. They climbed onto the first forest slope where he saw the biggest forest flower in the world which is a native to that area having collected some water from the early morning downpour. For every few meters, they have to stop to clear the long hanging plant matter which serves as ropes for forest dwellers. Then the leader said, please report any strange sound or any strange object which you are not sure of, never should you see it as the border to us as in here the best way of safety is collective security. Serpentine creatures like snakes sometimes may be hanging over heads and under the forest cover just waiting to strike. Is that okay man? To which he answered Yes, Sir... When the newly recruited staff from Africa press down the switch in an attempt to ring the bell, other Care Providers signal that it's time for supper; the kitchen staff make hand gestures to press home their demands that food is ready. One by one the Occulus quest was removed as several others were smiling, happy, and wished they were left alone out there but that was not the expression on the face of Tony Wood, the robbery team head.

Their medications were poured onto the serving plate for each person according to their needs, as water was served. Once men and women owned their ways, strength, and life now being taken care of like toddlers in a German kinder-garten. In such a Care home should tell you not even one among them is poor as each has more than two million dollars to his or her name and other investments on the London stock exchange. Some not they have no children or family to care for them in their homes but just, but all are busy and such care is the best option for their case. The headsets were all plug in for extra power and with feeding going on after medication, the soft sweet classical music was heard at the background, from Beethoven, Mozart and the likes. The Facility manager called for updates on drugs or medicines and also went round inspecting each room air supply and safety before they call it a day for another set of teams to pick up.

With global giants like Amazon, Face book, Twitter, Shopify, Instagram and the likes justling for a large market share of the Metaverse; soon all international and conti-nental shows like Miss Universe, Miss world, BET Award, Vodaphone Urban Music Award, Bollywood Film festival and many other shows will be screened on the Occulus Quest Vr making all who wish to be there, to be there after paying just a token to feel all the drama, motion and sensa-tion that has to be consumed. As such, any social person irrespective of the location on earth or in space can say "I was also there... "to be the ultimate words of expression, any who wants to stand out; have to be different this time. After thirty minutes of feeding and with the classical music play to put them to sleep, Rawlings and Wood the only two who can stand up on their own and to take some steps without any assistance were seen standing up and looking around like students on excursion. Like jewels under protection from their second owner, they were wheeled into their rooms one after the other only for sleep to whisper well into their ears and steal them away.

Then the arrival hall where there were more kisses than couples in love, more handshakes than businessmen around a negotiating table, more exchange of goodwill and hope than a religious faith exchange, and several sensations of peace and goodwill compared to the Christmas seasonal greetings. What else matters? The kind of people in the Arrival Hall are directly proportional in attitude to the Departure Hall and life here is good. Hugs and warm embraces, tears of joy, and big graceful looks from friends and family. Although the tour had just begun, all participants wanted to stay a bit longer to see what each airplane would pour out into the hall.

Hello... Sally yelled at Sandra who for all these while has never seen Sally's presence as a member of the group. They went further with each given another three hundred meta-lights to be able to comprehend what lies ahead of them. The team was split into two, with one visiting the airport maintenance unit and the other the Aviation watch tower. The aviation watch tower has three shift teams and each team is composed of twelve technical workers contacting and receiving any air plane which enters the air space of the country. You see, the work of the tower is so important that a slight mistake can cause more than fifty people to perish in a wild air crash either on the tarmac or in the air, as such after every one hour of work or communicating with the inbound planes, they take a thirty minutes break and such is the plan in here. More than three hundred planes are in the air space of the country at every given time either crossing over the country, about to land or leaving their country. And this is the nerve center and the place where they take their stand; you see those who work here are equally served with enough vacation such that all is well and all acts well to fit in.

Well, as you can see; three plans are on their way and they will land with just one hundred- and twenty-seconds interval and with those on the ground will leave every one minute.

At maintenance side the other group was busily climbing the stairs which leads to the kitchen which serves about eight thousand workers every shift as about thirty-two thousand people calls this place working place from cleaners, office workers, technicians, technologist, airside workers, port side workers, accountants, engineers, doctors and nurses, drivers, pilots and air crew, students on attachments and many others. This is a community where some meet their wives and husband and others to meet old school mates, what is wanted down here... just name it and this community can help out. Typically, the mechanical shop and hangers have more than six thousand tools and almost a million screws to work with either on aircraft or other physical structure around. Any question please...?

So, who is the head making sure all works well or well fit in? Sir Lord Dorson and Cynthia Daniels as his assistant. The airport has its own power supply system and separate from the city of London, water and sewage service, police and fire department and a judge coming from the justice department to help with international crimes and diplomatic stuff.

When the third nurse or care giver put on one of the Occulus Quest Vr, I wished I knew what she was thinking about as she arrived in that small country called Ghana in

West Africa and even deeper into their justice system and at cell number sixteen A where her elder brother has been for close to thirteen months from drug trafficking. The Ghanaian justice system sentenced Kobby to five years behind bars for selling drugs to some section of youths in one of the local areas of the country as the charge says. Either that is true or not, only God can tell … but then had she listened to mama before her death, such a punishment in an African prison will never come to pass.

Kobby was place in a small and well room about ten meters by three meters cell room and well packed with eleven other individuals where they are locked inn or go to bed at five o'clock afternoon and gets up at six o'clock the following morning. The twelve inmates all from different parts of the country and different crime background slept side by side in a dry and dirty floor infected with insects such as bedbugs and black African mosquitoes flying and biting all in there, what a wild state created for a human being? The high temperature, poor ventilation and lack of good cloths have made several among them to develop strange skin rushes which no doctor or dermatologist is coming to check or work on it. And bathing is done once in three days without detergents due to water conservation.

You see in Ghana there is only two kinds of accommodation system, yes, the whole country for that matter. Never mind about their so-called presidential Palace called Jubilee House, the State House, the prime locations such as East Cantoment, Airport West and Airport East, various Royal Palaces, Trasacco and even Villaggio… again there are other locations such as Nima, Madina, Sodom and Gomorrah, and even Tip-toe Lane residency in Nkrumah Circle also in

Accra rea and thousand-thousand villages across the landscape of the country. Accommodation is in two categories; it is about the State Sponsored Accommodation System (SAS) which the people Russian will it Gulag and the Americans will call Prison and the other is the Paid Accommodation System (PAS). With (PAS), one is free to be at where he or she choose to be, eat what he wants and be with who he or she wishes to be with but then basic needs like water, electricity and accommodation is paid for with cash and even if free it has been paid for by somebody ahead of time. That is not so for the State Sponsored Accommodation System (SAS) where when to sleep, where to sleep, how to sleep, what to eat, when to eat and even what to wear are all dictated to you by the state through the Jailer who is paid every month with allowances to do so. And this is what Kobby has found himself in.

The Medium Prison facility build to hold four thousand currently holds thirty-six thousand inmates and occupying more than seventy thousand hectors of land with about twenty-one feet tall well-fortified walls and sharp razors not just to cut open but inflict painful wound and even given you tetanus in response engulfs the facility with two-thousand and six hundred jailers on watch for every passing second of the day as they run a twelve-hour shift system for their monthly pay. The (SAS) is divided in to sections fit for the kind of crime committed as cell block E and F are for the hardened criminals who will see freedom in the next coming century and would kill any should they get closer. Currently they are about eight hundred in total with some killing their girlfriend, killing police and military men on night watch duty.

Cell block A and B for those spending between six months to just a year clear and are mild despite some tamed after getting there. Kobby and others are in Cell block D and even so, the physical conditions are enough to call it hell on earth. She was given the electronic right virtually to visit every cell or holding room and comparing it to the offices of the jailer, she began to feel uncomfortable as tears began to drop down her cheeks and yelled, oh man born of a woman, how have you lead your life and what is the ways forward?

The heat, poor ventilation even at night, mosquitoes at work, bedbugs on special diet, overcrowding and poor nutrition should be able to make any coming from this holding area to repent if not change his mind. But there was a huge open area which is only accessed at noon time for walk and keep fit and that is the period where foreign prisoners like Kobby are targeted for harm like how Thomas was killed with bare hands by six gangs within the prison system as he could not provide two cigarettes sticks as a token for his short stay.

His lifeless body was discovered after almost six hours as no weapons were used in the act and those who saw dared not talk about it... she crossed over to the female area where those there upon seeing her asked her for money which she did not give, well they asked her to walk out and that was that. The female cells were dirty and smelled too but all in there were cool.

Sarah, with just two meta-cedi on her meta-card, has seen and experienced a whole lot of new experience in the comfort and privacy of her work side.

TERMINALS

The internet has its own rules and regulations which any who dares plugs into it must obey but how many people obeys those rules even in Europe or America? How many even know such rules exist and where can it be located at all? But does it apply to all and if all what about minors watching cartoons next week with or without their parents? Can anybody who is reading this book name any without referring to any book or Professor Google? Can you do that huh?

The following rules are what the Meta-Quart has been able to put together for the first degree or first level of operation called the meta-Das which provides all dwellers, passersby, and stakeholders of the meta-zone to operate and cooperate with all sorts of meta-lights. The meta-terra power may be said to be biased but then it aims to make sure each person is given the needed energy park or meta-data to go about doing his or her work, duty, travels, events, and associations. The lower laws are as follows;

1. No bullying, Insults, or threats.
2. No identity theft and exchange of Meta-card.
3. No exchange of meta-data and data coupling of any kind.
4. Meta-light is the single corridor all must follow.
5. Tolerance is the next watchword to make you go places.
6. Exist and report odd issues to the Meta-Quart for redress.
7. Sincerity and responsibility are the name of the game.

There she sits, in the all glamour and pouch sitting room of the American ambassador residence in Ghana; she emptied the half a litters bottle of Pepsi with sugar free cake after a long day of talks and meetings with ambassadorial stuff despite being a diabetic patient and for where she is, her physician isn't going to know and that is a fact. She stretched her legs only to reach out for the Occulus Quest which arrived at the residence two weeks ago from Amazon. He Excellency Nancy Nordson, the ambassador of United State of America to Ghana placed the device on and in less than sixty seconds, there she was in the company of her grandchildren in Wyoming which the very last time she saw them was five years ago in Knoxville. The warm hugs override a firm handshake as Nancy the youngest among them began to shed tears of seeing grandma again with Frankie and Josh looking on patiently; after almost two minutes of emotional hugs, they held hands as all walked into the sitting room to watch a new Netflix family movie called "There We Go Again". They sat down in the cool and spacious room as with small pillows, popcorn and a bottle of

Fanta each, each person settled in for a smooth ride and that is what an American family is.

Calm and quietness midst gratefulness fell upon all and unity was all around till the movie was almost ending when Frankie opened up, only to complain to Grandma how Josh took his money back at school. Stop yadding, stop yadding about me Josh protested sharply. Well, well, it looks like we have issues on our hands; tell me what is happening with you boys? Grandma requested... he took my money Frankie pressed on with Josh saying I will pay back, so stop talking out loud man!!

Well, I have some Chinese friends who introduced me to a new game which is played with money, thinking I would make a good win; I ended up losing and those Chinese boys went away with my money. I had to use Frankie's money and promised to pay it back when I made some money on my own. That is where we got to. Humm, but did you make Frankie aware before using the money knowing it's for him huh? No grandma... Josh answered in a low tone as he looked away from her direction. He must pay up and pay it fast, Frankie said gaining more power as Grandma was warming to her side.

And how much are we talking about here, grandma asked. Two dollars, Frankie sounded. Well, we also agreed that every passing week that he does not pay attracts half a dollar more to be paid, and from my checks, it has been five weeks now. With that said Grandma burst into a wild two-minute laughter when Frankie added the half-dollar part during their agreement. Okay, you people are full of witty minds, wow... but how or who schooled you on the additional money that is interesting at this stage in life huh? Was it at school or... grandma I learned that in a movie last summer, and it's a great way to make money... Frankie sounded...

With the Occulus quest, you can meet up with any friend or family member anywhere in the world as long as he or she is on the plate form at the same period. In the American embassy or on the list of embassy staff is the able male Office clerk called Arul Dasuki, whose other twin is beautiful Anan Dasuni all being Sri Lankan citizens. Arul Dasuki after his Commonwealth scholarship education in Ghana decided to stay and is now with a family of four including his Ghanaian wife Senna. He stepped onto the electronic scene only to order an Oculus on Amazon and submitted the address of his twin sister Dasuni in Sri Lanka after making her aware of what was yet to arrive. Despite the poor financial gain and bleak economic outlook of the country, the country Ghana is two to three steps ahead compared to Sri Lanka whose economic outlook is in the waters of the Indian Ocean awaiting to be drowned in the deep.

The Sri Lank economy which has heavily depended on Chinese loans and bonds, help, and advice are as weak and helpless as a day-old baby sucking its thumb. The country's inflation is high and so high that the central bank has begun the daily printing of paper money to woo the general public and the total monetary reserve for imports for the country is just three weeks. It has three point two billion United States dollars to pay in less than three months to those the country owns in bonds payment, capital investment, and loans. Currently, the streets of the capital Colombo are teaming with a long chain of humans standing to buy bread, fuel, and access to potable water. Several shelves have no imported and perishable products for sale and private citizens and other individuals have begun leaving the city center only to take a trip to their home villages, country side and other places far from sight as the government workers who have no option keeps afloat and looking as the government scrambles for help from India and Singapore; which had they made that move earlier on, instead of allying with China would have help the economy immensely. The military whose leadership have become like a sitting duck are silent, firmly stuck to their guns which chances are; will never spit out a bullet but have their well-pressed uniforms as a sign of loyalty to the state and people no matter what.

After just five days, Dasuni called up her brother only to report the safe arrival of the gadget and to let him know what was at stake in the country and it looked like it was a good thing for him to stay out of the country to trade help with mama who is weak with age and almost a century old. She set the device in place and lo and behold was able to pick the right bottom as she arrived at the gateway of her brother in Ghana for some talk; a reunion after almost twelve years of no see. The hug was wild and powerful as the children looked on with a bit of surprise but then who is that and where does she come from? The children asked their papa... she was welcome home and well into the African Sri Lankan family as Senna served her with some water after placing the Hisense television remote in her hands to kick off her relaxation.

He introduced the children to their long-lost auntie and Dasuni to her nephew and nieces making the children ask, are you the one we have been speaking to on the telephone? Yes, please she sounded... she looked at the Ghanaian wife and asked, what was so special about this rough boy that you took him as a husband? Senna smiled and as if not wanting to talk began to spill the tone of information onto the floor of the living room. When I was still a girl, a strange-looking man whom I came across on a means of public transport was advising a lady and what I gathered is what has brought me this far. Dasuni smiled and adding; Oh... so you are a spy, right? No, really Senna answered... and the man began, in the adaptations of a man and woman, women can adapt far better to men in the relationship. As such as a lady, learn to glue yourself to a man who loves you more than you. For chances are; as the days become weeks and months become years, the love of men reduced per time compared to a woman.

The man would see younger and better-looking women than you and some women who have hard earn cash than you can possibly get. And the conclusion of the matter is, will he blink his eye or not? Will he stick to you or not and will he as a man commit further to you or not? And during all these whiles, women keep their commitments and love in that marriage as long as they have shelter and food on the table. Women in general increases their affection in relationship; as the affection and love of men reduces, and that is a fact. the sideways movement is directly proportional to the times and events as stake. And when I checked, his love for me was just in the level and measurement of the affection scale; so, here we are now madam.

The African gods were at work but the invokers of the black African Voodoo were at loggerheads with themselves over who has the right to call upon the gods of the land. The movie was at it again, as village elders wanting peace and preservation of the environment were at war with the leaders of the youth who wanted development and jobs hence the decision to sale the land to the Chinese entrepreneur who want it for a factory or the South Korea investor wanting to used it for a hospital was at large. As the twelve elders who are above the age of seventy-five evoke the power of their gods at midnight, the youth also call upon the same god by the day before noon for help. The all-men activity was on and heating up as the ladies and women of the village looks on like a lamp being taken to a slaughter house as the village customs prevents them from such decisions.

In the middle of the whole act is the local government official whose acts are a reflection of either having taken money from the investors to help them or wanting to pull the deal off for a hefty financial reward at the end of the day. So, who will break the truce as spirituality have been introduced to mortal affairs of man?

One hour to close of banking hours, the bank staff were almost in a rush asking and calling people as if they are in harry to somewhere but not, even the bank's chief accountant was up and walking moving to customers asking them if they have been served or not. The whole atmosphere in the banking hall was racing ahead of the time to serve all clints and to start the act of balancing their books for the end of the day when the robbers set off from six building away from the bank as all were not expecting such a guest until it happened. The five team of robbers with weapons mysteriously gotten from the British armed forces middle man on the dark web, they spared off only to hit the road in a calm vehicular pace like any other as they bypassing two police cars and a military van without any clue to show that they are evil and armed to the teeth. Dexter was behind the steering wheels homing down the road and plotting every possible escape plane in his head, a head which failed him when it comes to school making him a school dropout at the junior high level some twelve years back making the world of casino to adopt him. The banking hall was left with two more clients to serve when a red American model Toyota Tacoma truck pulled into the drive way packing closer to the entrance of the bank when the first person with black full-face mask shot at the bank security officer with a silent pistol and that was it. The four other men joined him as in a swift move entered the banking hall as asked for the bank manager who was in the toilet at that moment, the bank's accountant was shocked as he lay on the floor with being asked to do so.

Well, hope the banking day was good, Sampson the son of an Italian immigrant some twenty years back pulled out a black bag with a set of instructions one of them to the bank tellers was drop every available cash including coins in to this bag and be quick about it. Should any press an alarm or should any police team show up, I will shoot you in the head. The first two tellers did as was instructed as within two minutes; close to two million pounce sterling was bag and other staff were adding more. The twelve-banking staff were all asked to sleep with their eyes closed as Tony a native British taking their cell phones from their hands and by that time Taiwo another son of an immigrant from Nigerian who is a computer specialist hijack the computing system of the bank making all other possible alarms and sound to freeze up. The bank manager was pulled out from where he was as he was taken to the bank's vault which hold secrets and documents best to be kept in such a place. Like a grave yard, both inside and outside the bank was silent even the security man who was shoot was pulled in as the pool of blood on the floor was cleaned up by the bank's cleaning staff under the orders of the robbers.

The driver was calm, silent and still sitting in the car with the engine still on, as if not part of what is unfolding. With the combination of codes, the manager cooperated as within seventy seconds the massive big vault was open as Tony and Sampson reached for solid gold, diamonds, other Jewells whose designs such as swastika, lotus, tiger and tiny Lord Ganesh tells it belongs to Indians in and around the city. With a huge load of gold or fit to be called gold-load, the team walked out of the bank with close to three million pounce sterling notes and two hundred thousand new coins from the five tellers. Sampson led the way as others followed and Taiwo promising the banking staff that the computer system will work again after just one hour. The four robbers worked like a surgical without flaws and they threw the money and jewels into the bucket of the truck, hopped into the car and drove away like celebrities on the red carpet. When all was gone and things returning to normalcy, the bank manager picked the banks phone wanting to inform the authorities but the line was dead, even the internet of the bank was up and doing yet still freeze up.

Well after leaving the heavy traffic area, they zapped into a building only to change cars and now driving in a hospital ambulance with the hazard lights turned on except the alarm system as they head away from the lanes leading to the hospitals. The jewels almost amounting to sixteen million pounce sterling was gone and as they keep moving the branched off the NW2 Highway and escaped without a trace. And this robbery was the sixth job under the belt of Tony, Dexter, Taiwo who have been doing this for close to five years after the casino and the wild life of drugs did not pay them well. Adnan, a metallurgist student who dropped out in the third year of his studies join a gang of petty robbers but in each episode of robbery is given less than expected as such switch sides twice till, he came across Tony in a friend's party last spring. He is now a British whose parents were all born in Iran only to arrive in London on a tourist visa some twenty-five years ago. But Sampson, also a British now was once an Italian and a master in the lock business following in the footstep of his father who was and still is a locksmith minding his own business in Leeds.

As a team, this robbery was their first job which is rewarding them with millions of pounce sterling and that is what I call power-job with only one person killed. And the London atmosphere was wild as most Londoners were surprised of the new development as the Police station about seven blocks away did not even have a clue during the robbery process. The whole process was computer linked and computer induced as the Nigerian computer mind was a perfect march freezing the entire computer system of the bank.

Inasmuch as much as the sun is the center of the solar system; the art of stealing the sun will be far different from the art of stealing the moon, one has to follow some basic rules such as never get caught in the process, do it at a period when it's not shining bright, push it four degrees left and six degrees right for a perfect dash away. Use to some of the motivational words Tony tells his fellow team players three days before every bank robbery. Either that hold water or not, time will be the factor as every robbery is a work of art where your first move can be your very last... the sun is the money, the onlookers are the London Police and they are the brave partakers....

In the robbery of Finch Bank after just two years from the last perfect job, Dexter was shoot twice to the chest making him bleed profusely like a burst water line under pressure and in less than sixty seconds lost the company of the group and losing the bag full of money to the advancing terrorist police as the cash was on. Taiwo, the Nigerian took was the one with the wheels driving to the best of his ability and swiping wild through the traffic and pushing others around and off the road with the Ford truck like Lego being cast off. He took the first turn right, then left only to meet another wild team of police, he rams one of the cars of the police killing its occupant in a hard bang and drove off as the second police car reversed to chase them making the city dwellers to panic and almost making the whole thing look like a Hollywood movie scene. With several gun bullets rushing after them, the car tank was hit but did not cause an explosion instead the car began to lose fuel with them knowing till after thirty minutes hot run on the high way leading out of London to the north where the car stopped and they jumped off and into the side of the road. They shot an approaching driver in a blue Toyota sedan car killing him with just a bullet to his head and took the car from after pull him onto the main road. Not knowing where next as what he is doing isn't his role in the whole activity, Taiwo took the right turn only to start heading towards the city of London again and that was where things got rough for them. The cashing police team with a city authority did not perform any U-turn but drove against the traffic in their best of ability as they shoot and one of their bullets drove its head into the neck region of Adnan and in less than half a minute the back seat of the car was filled with blood and help was coming from nowhere.

The bags containing the money was sprayed and painted with blood taking it out will be a risk as any can make a trace to them and even so the cash was on. In a sharp work of surprise, Tony the team leader forcefully opened the door at the back of the car seat only to push the lifeless body of Adnan as if to say now we have no use for you. Taiwo kept doing his part till they branched right and into an area in the city where mostly people don't visit. A new team of police welcomed them with shooting and other works of force and when they stopped Taiwo stopped, a stray bullet forced its way into the side of his ribs making breathing difficult and signal them to move on as he sat silent and without any extra move in the driver's seat with the police advancing upon his position. They others allowed themselves to be buried by the disuse factory building taking just one bag load of money. The first police officer who got to his position fearing it's a trap, opened fire and killing the computer giant right there.

The seasoned Tony was still alive and doing just fine except Sampson who in attempt to jump a pile of metals had his left leg cut making him bleed and with that may lead to their capture. Finally with an unbearable pain and difficult in walking, he stopped asking Tony to go and keep the money till the meet again somewhere for his cut of the cash. The dogs, the police dogs were at work smelling, picking scents, sniffing, detecting their whereabout and behold there he is, laying on the bar floor soaked with fresh human blood and what else can he do. The first two black security dogs who got to him did not just seize him but were on the offensive fighting him, attacking him from the neck region and the chest, biting, tearing, pulling and in less than two minutes he was well washed with his own blood as those vicious dogs caused his beating hear to stop, the dogs killed him before the police got to his position. The huge dog seized him to the neck, pressing and in the process preventing air and blood from getting to where its required and that was his end, The Italian born British was dead and gone. The robbery at the Finch Bank was about six million cash and as it stands now have lost all except what is in the possession of Tony which is about two hundred and ten thousand pounce sterling which should that get to the London casino, will run out in just one hour.

And all was gone, a bad day which should they be Chinese citizens who have dedicated fortune teller, the fortune teller would have made them aware to stay put till another time or period.

Well, what else matters? there he is, I mean the now old Tony the bank robber in his late seventies, as he lay silently in his bed with a brain and spinal cord injury which he sustained from a normal shopping trip as currently he is being taken care off like a royal and in all his dealings, was never arrested or found out. The old Tony still dreams and wishes to outwit the meta sphere by robbing them of a multi-million meta-cedi perhaps wanting to check their able-ness, security system and ability to execute judgement.

Notwithstanding his little knowhow; he has been dreaming of how to replace himself when he is gone in the way of other masters of the art of robbery but more important is how to get the next winning team to game up on the meta as the metapol seems to be a bit shy to stop people, asking and checking their ID. Even as he lay silently in his warm bed nurtured by Care givers well paid to do so; he has twenty-six million pounce sterling tuck away in an unmarked plot in one of the old grave yards which has been closed for use for over thirty-two years now which lies east of London but as at now can't find his way back and the authorities don't even have a clue over who he is and what he was.

In a conversation with Rawlings, he asked so, this meta, what is its soft spot? And how rich can one be in the meta? At least for where we are now, we know people who are worth billions of dollars and families owning as much as a trillion dollars to their family name what is your take on that? I don't know and all that I hope for is my fair share of the cake and what can be-can be, am old and chances are that I may leave here anytime from now and without saying good bye. Come on man, grow up... Rawlings responded to his words. Well, not to upset you man but I here there is a degree of operation in the meta, is the highest degree being like having a sort of security clearance before getting there huh? I think that is called meta-Qark. Tony requested to know...

Rawlings began; am not the originator or the creator of the meta, for I am just a user like you are, just explore it and bring me a word should you find something I know not man. Or better still mind your own business... is that okay!!

The Care home cook surfaced with some meals which upon tasting by a normal person will be strange and odd; and the meals are as follows, pepper-free, salt-free soup, oil-free tomatoes stew, carbohydrate-free rice, vegetables and fish only meals which is all that, that patient has been taking for breakfast, lunch and supper for close to five years now and others in a cup as such patients are not to take solid foods. The morning eating session alone is a three-hour activity not as if they are eating like an emperor or slow in nature but just that it is how things have become for them after years of several hard life which paid off but in their current state; can't enjoy what they have earned. The three-hour block of eating began with the care givers being as active as they can be feeding those with needs and supervising those who can feed themselves a bit. The last group is the kind of patients whose meal is in a paste form or liquid and they must be feed in bits using a cup as the food if poured down their throat. The once men and women who were movers and shakers of their era now sits like toddlers in a kindergarten class, they are rich with huge investment, hard earn cash and just can't enjoy it as with some their children are so busy to pay them a visit.

THE SHY HILLS

A type two diabetic patient with dementia which is an odd occurrence to possibly happen to a full grown man, he sat calmly as his investment at the bank keeps doubling and rising like a wet flour spiked with yeast before baking in the oven. The nurse pulled out the syringe and needle only to inject insulin in his body through the left thin without saying a polite "sorry" to smoothen the pain. But then, what else is wanted in this world of challenges, pain, disappointment, mistrust and unfaithfulness. Twenty- eight years ago when working as an able and stable civil servant, he run across a handsome member of the British Parliament on the list of House of Commons and a very frank man in his dealings with his fellow man util that day. The lower Lord of things had two chemical companies constituting chemicals for construction such as adhesive, paints of all colours and kinds, water sealants, vanish and abrasives.

The company fashioning these chemicals is called Slide Tone Base Chemicals based in an old industrial plot and attracting the authorities but then there is a catch to it. With the capacity to produce six thousand litters of chemicals per week, the company reports just five thousand and six hundred litters of per month. Mr. Alex James Hyde as a public servant and inspector of public facilities under the Mayor of London he crossed carpets with more than seven thousand factory operators and owners per month and for each the rules are laid down and for some until the police or the law was applied nothing was done. With some characters, they offered for a sit down talks which was driving towards offering money to the inspectors to forget what was wrong and this is what Alex did not like about his job. As an inspector, several ill-people will want to offer cash for neglect which some say other inspectors are very wise and cooperative compared to him in line of duty. Alex in the company of three others surfaced without a prior notice and asked who is in-charge. They introduced themselves after pulling out their fill which contains some check list ready to capture date when Sir John Long interrupted and asking them to meet with him first in his office which was granted.

He requested for time and asked for personal copy of key indicators for which the answer was no, not allowed.

He soon began to spill out his credentials and where he has been t and who he knows but even so that did not shake Mr. Hyde from his firm feet except his other staff members. He walked away, and without a word began to inspect, touch and to key in information about the facility starting from the outside structure as other team members were still in talks with the owner... the other inspectors were almost warming into the advancing with a sum of thirty thousand pounce sterling to either under report or report that all is alright when Alex surfaced and making all know there are open cracks within and the surface of the main pillars holding the structure. The two leaders faced off, in an exchange of insults as each was right and all were wrong. The inspecting team went away having taken records and lost a huge sum of money which is three times their monthly salary with bonuses. The fishbone as others within his rank at work call him, Alex is so firm and so religious that he will not accept even a pounce sterling from a man to alter his work for a degree, and again does not accept free lunch from either male or female coworker. That is the legendary fish bone... despite not being liked by his coworkers as a boss and coworker, nothing can be done to him until transferred or his retirement is due.

In the Meta, there are three degrees or levels of glory and each degree has its benefits as one will only be moved or inherit a higher degree or level based on his or her achievements, good deeds, service, and knowledge leading to a higher meta-light and hopefulness within the Meta. The degrees are as follows;

Meta-Das - 1st Degree or level
Meta-dash - 2nd Degree or level
Meta-Qark - 3rd Degree or level

From the first degree to the next will warrant good behavior such as no bullying, no insults, no harassment of any female avatar, no fanny comments and mocking at people, no breaking the rules of the meta, no abuse of children and old people on the platform, no rape or gang rape and finally destruction of private and public property. When an abuser or harasser insults a lady without any provocation, the Metapol pops up from nowhere taking action with the help of the meta-zone by reducing the person or the offender's meta-light to half of its original size and further banning him for using or visiting the platform for the next twenty- four hours. In a wilder case or offensive nature and should the victim, make a report to the Meta-Quart the Meta-Zone will issue a statement and set up a committee of inquiry as soon as possible.

The girl was taken to the trauma unit of the metapol as physicians were assigned and the university authorities were equally informed giving them extra meta-data about what just happened. After almost ten minutes of extra tabulation, Alex was released but then his meta-card was swiped across the charge machine taking every needed information from him including fingerprints, eye color, and other genetic information. In such a case he as a witness will not be charged but will be again his name that such a thing happened and he saw it and did nothing about it. The three American citizens were arrested after a struggle with the Metapol claiming they had done nothing wrong and, since vacation, they had never been to the campus despite being students, they arrived at the police department where what happened was replayed to them silencing them in less than a minute. And how will this case be judged?

Despite worried about his data being in the hands of those people, he checked in to another zone that same mid-afternoon, after changing the clothes of his avatar; this is what he first saw boldly written on a billboard by the seventy-second street in New York;

- Elements of the metaverse
- Gaming Digital assets
- Device independence Tokens
- Digital markets Entertainment
- Digital currency Online shopping
- Workplace Social media
- Digital humans Image processing

He stopped and began to read from point to point making sure he digested every point and even looked for meanings why such and what is in it for him as a regular user of the metaverse.

That is the property of the Crown Prince of Bahrain, a royal whose deep pocket has no limit like that of Saudi Arabia, does that ring a bell huh? He purchased that three hundred by five hundred land for close to two hundred and twenty United States dollars only allowed to leave it to grow weeds with no one knowing what he was planning to do on the land. Currently, it has birds, butterflies, insects, and even some wild ducks doing their own thing. He has a wide collection of mansions, buildings, and other private items across the meta and chances are he may sell them off when times get tough but when will such a thing happen knowing the kind of land he rules over? Currently; he has a kind of meta-light making him occupy a graceful sport in the second degree of the meta where all those there are told either have earned it through security clearance and good behavior or purchased it at a prime rate. Mumm, so here too the rich and resourceful still call the shots over poor individuals as they stretch their hands to pick all the lineup prime property of the metaverse; what a new world. Okay, so how is the documentation done here?

When a purchase is displayed or announced by the meta-light; several other meta-agencies are noticed as the Council of Tokens underwrites a document ahead of time pending, he who will pay for it. And with payment done, the meta-card of the person is reassigned to such property and named as such. The art of acquisition is as simple as ABC just that, the monthly or year property rate is what is killing. But are you planning of obtaining one huh? The man asked him for which he replied no. The once and still Fish Bone hearing the mountain high price began to walk away from what he just heard from the man whom he thinks what he is saying is worth thinking about.

He walked around and kept moving from point to point as if he was the newly appointed surveyor to survey the whole land as no green plants, flowers, animals, or even water-like insects were seen; in fact, it's a barren land with its unique coastal beauty as it meets the open sky-blue ocean and equally fit to contest other places of the world in a neck-to-neck competition. And when the sunshine rises from the east of the land, it had no mercy upon the small dry, and tree-less land, as the saying goes; the sun shines upon all irrespective of your character, deeds, and aspirations for once day breaks it will certainly do what it has to do. The sunshine which always subdues the fauna and flora of Africa equally does the same thing to this orphan land between the continent of Africa and the subcontinent of Arabia with no mercy and heating the small land fifteen minutes before that of Africa as all inhabitants living there have never said anything nice over the sun harsh and unfriendly ways over the years yet they have nowhere to go.

Then at the western section of the land was another strange kind of tree, big trunks and some branches holding a few red-like leaves rising about ten meters about the soil surface, and even so, there were no flying birds seen around. Surprisingly, no snakes, scorpions, or even harmful spiders like those seen in the wild part of Texas in the United States of America. And despite a unique environment, tourism was zero a good mark to preserve the land but a bad mark for the economy of the locals living there as their looks tells poverty is no too far from where they stand as nutrition is but a challenge.

In a slow walk, Alex began to dash away from that exotic land and soon appeared on the street of Texas just close to a gas station and from afar saw a struggle between two men and a woman due to what he experienced earlier took some steps back and would not like to be part of it. The three avatars of people he knows but once decided to stay away from never realized what is going on; it was the Avatar of Hannah one of the Care home registered nurses who every morning pushes hospital drugs down the throat of patients like a military commander on parade without patience and mercy as every patient in the Care home is twice her age and with what she does, makes her unpopular and disrespectful to many but each person or all combine have no strength and energy of their own to fight or shout at her attitude towards them. As Alex Hyde stands afar for what is unfolding; The talking man in blue top clothes and black jeans holds the woman in all green clothes from top to down only to push her onto the floor with other passersby looking away and bystanders stopping to see and video what was happening without breaking the fight or stopping the guys. The next guy in all her jeans clothes kicked her to the head with his right black boots as he rolled on the floor each charged towards her like predators on the wild wilder beast on the Serengeti of East Africa. Stop, stop, stop it... please have mercy, stop were the words of the registered Nurse rolling on the bare floor as her nakedness was for all to see, wild or angry guys kept hitting hard at her for a crime she committed in the other world called Earth.

Hannah was in tears but was more in the pan than the tears as there were several bruises on her face and blood stains on her left arm and very dirty to move on to where she was heading. And well before the guys stopped or were satisfied, the Metapol arrived without anyone calling them, stopped the fight, and arrested them as each was handcuffed and taken away as Hannah was carried away in an ambulance. The avatar of Tony Wood and one of the newly introduced patients in the name of Jonathan Jimmy Snow were taken away. As for Hannah, the nurse; the act of doing her work amidst the act of giving morning medications to the patients has led to all this, a classic occupational hazard right there. The avatars of Tony and Jimmy were placed under sanction for thirty days, meta-light reduced and their advancement to the next degree of the meta will require a higher-level security clearance as their case was readily placed onto the Meta-blaqq list of wild, unpleasant, and dangerous people in the category of murderers and bank robbers across every operating agency on the metaverse.

Also, the Metapol arrested or detained twenty-two others who did not stop the attack on the poor woman but were taking pictures or videoing what was happening from several youths, adults, and one journalist thinking he was taking proceedings to report to his media house as the poor woman was hurting and may get killed by those guys. After all these, Alex was free from any blame but upon seeing those involved was so sorry for Hannah and even so, was unwilling to get closer or get his name on the charge sheet as, as of now his meta-light has been down written and it will be so for the next six months as some privilege on the meta has been taken away from him.

Meanwhile on that very day; Mary in company with three others wheeled in a new female patient who had spent close to half a century in Idaho as a farmer raising animals together with her late husband and six children who all are moved out and currently working in several locations across the world, especially South East Asia. As indicated on her transfer letter which is attached to her medical history or file, she is a type two diabetic with a brain injury that she sustained in a car crash having received five surgeries with three and half years of stay at the hospital. Finally, her children have given the green light to keep her here with a surety to pay her upkeep of about nine and half thousand dollars a month stay package including upkeep, medications, care, and other facility use. Calm and silent like a baby he looks around and at faces for the first time not knowing what will happen who will love her and when will she leave this human cage called body for free and endless joy. The eighty-eight years old woman had her neck and head pointing to one position like a stiff-necked people under the direction of Moses of old; whose plan and aim is to go against the word of God as written in the Old Testament of the bible. From a distance, the only thing any can see and conclude that she is not all that well is her fast and constant blinking of the eye due to the neck surgery which as of now nothing can be done about.

Mary was the very person feeding with the bottle as Tracy supervised those with the ability to eat on their own; the meal time is always a spectacle as any who come across these once able and masters of their own now being taken care of like babies tell a whole story to the proud, high and lofty person, vulgar and snobbish youth and even a healthy in the body that, there comes a time when things change and luck may not be on your side as you need somebody to take care and be by you no matter what, as such if you have good health you are in control. Hannah first went to old and fray Jimmy who is full of himself in the meta and before taking the first spoon to his mouth smiled as the poor Jimmy looked on. Well, the first spoonful of porridge went to his mouth, and slowly took it allowing it down his throat; feeding for close to seven minutes till she stopped only to move on to Tony.

The whole hall now was in the hands of the active beings in the person of the caregivers and two administrative workers jostling over the Oculus Quest VR as in who will pick what and with each planning where next to visit. Mary fixed the headset, followed by Margaret as Hannah looked on hopefully to the wild two who never let the wild side of things pass them by. They once met in Las Vegas where they have a saying that "What happens in Vegas stays in Vegas" holds but then, what were they up to or what were they doing there? As Tracy once said, she first picked up her boyfriend in the casino halls of Las Vegas and after just two weeks of fun and pleasure they broke up. That guy was a bad guy as she introduced her to the art of smoking and that nearly vanished her finances. She now goes by the saying smoking if for the rich list of the society. In white long lace clothes, she arrived on the red carpet of the German film festival where she was received by handsome males who took er to her seat after paying twelve meta-cedi to be in the twenty-second roll of the hall a few seats away from the VIP seats reserved for movie stars and the rich list who may show up. She wore a ten thousand meta-cedi lace and silk cloth designed by Masada Ventures a company owned by her brother who works in the fashion business in New York. Her all-clean pink footwear by Dass Apparel and handbag by Mark and Spencer was one in town.

While all these are happening for Mary, Margaret is seen in on top of her game as she pays her way to the front view of the basketball game between the LA Lakers and The Mavericks as each player picks on the opposing team member in a do or die match which the winner will not only pick the golden cup for keep but will dash away with a sum of eighty-six million dollars and the bragging rights for the next twelve months in and around the nation with nobody stopping them. Apart from the winning money, there is about one hundred and eleven million dollars in advertising cash and other lost cash which will fill the club's bank accounts in less than twenty-four hours from the end of the game that is if they are the winners. She saw and beheld the huge and tall guys who were on top of their game doing their own thing to bag that cash if academics couldn't help them, their skills and height would do the rest. Jay Brown the side striker for the Lakers kept hammering the Maverick with point after point as his eyes were glued to that cash called money too. Well before the break the La Lakers have sixteen points more compared to the Maverick who are having things difficult with the defenders and blockers at the back. During the short break and as per planed, twelve nice looking entertainers stepped onto the polished court where the treated the vast number of people about sixteen thousand plus with nice dancing moves and skills of movement as several other cast popcorn into their mouth. She soon spotted two Lebanese or Indian guys who after giving their money to the calm seated man with brown leather bag; walked away from with the hopes that their respective team will win hands down; well, it's just a game but it looks like people are betting with their money as it's a chance to increase their worth within the shortest possible time along the fun of wining.

Well before the second half went on, she dashed out to use the washroom and whilst in that process run across on of her school mate during her nursing school where they chat a bit and exchange numbers. The second part of the game began well before she arrived as the Lakers and the Maverick began to battle it out from side to side as every passing second is a vital opportunity. All things being equal; Hannah arrived at a lone sleeping botanical garden in the eastern cold part of the world where cleanliness and hygiene is a hallmark. She stepped into a clean, organized and crafted trees and plants under the supervision of Gino Hashimoto who for the past thirty-seven years have been in charge and alive with every growing plant in the garden which receives almost forty-five thousand visitors with fifteen percent coming from the country of Japan. The entrance of the garden stands an old Samurai tree which his believed to be about nine hundred years old and still alive and growing surrounded by some young trees less than two hundred years old. the light green and almost transparent waters of a pond filled with fishes and other aquatic plants is but a spectacle.

With winter approaching, no chirping bird was heard as the approached cold winds is a sharp reminder to all to take cover; the well planted and groomed white and yellow flowers are majestic, gracious and royal in its own fashion. After the first one hundred meters into the garden, a sudden open grace of flowers with sparkling petals is ready to suck pull inn, that is if you believe and truly know what is beauty. With looking down as she keeps her steps steadily moving forward, a white rabbit jumped crossed her path making her freak out but soon she was in a wild laughter.

The well-designed botanical garden even from a close look was like a computer art or out of this world. The beautiful Japanese architecture, the stone masonry and the symbols were enchanting and exotic to look upon. The two thousand and five hundred hector botanical garden is the highest and the coldest in the country which once belong to a local Lord who ruled about twenty-six years before the birth of Christ (BC). All by herself and knowing she is at a place where the respect for girls and women is high, she went about from point to point seeing and taking in all that she sees with thanks.

Margaret soon woke up for duty checks on all patients as it has been from time to time during sleep time; all was well as the beating lungs and hearts of patients were active and producing movement along with heat except Suzy. She tucked herself in a silent pose, never worried of the temperature in the room and had both eyes well opened but what does she see? Her head was well covered with a small cloth called bonnet to keep temperature stable, as her lips and face well moisturized like going for an event. Silent, motionless and stiff which any experience nurse can see from the way her neck holds her head at a fixed angle. Upon touch, she was cold despite the twenty-two degrees Celsius room temperature. Nurse Margaret called for Hannah who also asked for help from Mary and in less than a minute, there was a conclusion that she is gone, gone to her maker who made her. Suzy; the latest patient was clinically pronounced dead in less than twenty-four hours of her stay as at eleven past the top of the hour in the dead of the night. And that was the very first dead to be record for that very year. And when her medical history was fetched, it was written that; her remains would be donated to the John Hopkins medical school to be used as a teaching material for the medical students. The consulting physician was informed and she gave her remarks as stated in the patient's medical history and record.

ROYAL HABITS

When the music is good, it deserves to be played again is the saying on the dancing floors of the night club and so is the rhythm on the Meta.

He kept to his intensions as he has done in the real life being active, alert, humble and very selective to placed he choose to go and who he moves around with. Again; he avoided the enticing of other happy and will guys he comes across making sure he is the very one doing the picking of friends like stocks on the Wall Street and not the other way round. The events, location, duration of stay, intensions, activity and even what to spend his money on is buy his and not any other person he comes across. Never has the Metapol accused him of any wrong deeds, association or even a witness in any negative acts for all this while. As soon as he surfaced at the Prime Meridian Bistro, a team of Metapol surfaced in a clean and well dress uniforms began to approach him as Rawlings began to think of what is wrong with himself. In the middle of the team of all men was a medium height man with a brown wrapped paper like a scroll and upon reaching said; good day Sir, my name is Staff Sergeant Richard Tom Molls and by the orders of the Meta-Quart, your ways and efforts has been noticed and as a good citizen of the meta, it's the honor of the Meta-Zone to acknowledge you and to promoted to the second level or second degree in the meta called Meta-dash where you will occupy second region with enough meta-light to do more and also with the ability to return to the lower degree where you once was. Do you have any objections to this offer Sir?

Erhh, how much will that cost me? Rawlings relied sharply... it's a reward, it's a price as such; there is no financial component to that and there will be no social token such planting a tree or any social project. Can we say it's a 'Yes" ... year, yes for me Rawlings replied... Thank you and from now on you will be given an add-on meta-light of about eighty-eight terabyte and should you require more, please just request it and thank you very much sir. Just like they surfaced, the team went away without a trace as done in the meta and within two seconds he received a band on the upper part of his left arm as he slides into the new world with some new possibilities. He was welcomed by the beautiful tail of the long mountainous highlands of Chile sparsely populated with both animals and human beings. It is South America, its Latino, and it's a lonely place fit to be called the Switzerland of South America just that they speak fanny. The snow-white mountains are high, unforgiven with temperature, sharp rocks, and steep valleys to discourage any mountain climber but even so, mountainous goats were standing perfectly still at their sides.

They soon checked out only to check in at a new world wonder called the Panama Canal, a mechanical masterpiece of work and another testament that man was created in the image and character of God in terms of creation and industry.

Marco conducted him around from point to point as workers of the yard and other engineers responded to their visits in a timely fashion as given to Presidents and other diplomats on a working visit to such place from time to time... they saw the workings of the hydraulic compressors, water pumps, huge mechanical doors or gates as it closes and closes for water to raise the huge ship from point to point. The Chinese shipping line, Evergreen with the ability to carry about twenty-eight thousand containers soon arrived at the entry point where with tug boats and ropes, the huge metallic boat was gently assisted to enter the first holding area after the lock closed for water to pump or jerk the ship high which lasts about ten minutes. The second door was opened allowing the ship to move forward with the help of ropes and set up a small rail system that uses electricity from its generators to drive forward as it pulls the huge metal along. In a bit-by-bit fashion, the ship got to the last point where it entered another man-made water body called Gatun Lake which serves as a springboard to enter the vast blue ocean. After two and half hours watch of proceedings, they were offered lunch which as things were, he declined politely and asked for a boat ride to see the final entry point between the Gatun Lake and the vast ocean where the ships say good bye; which was granted.

Meanwhile at the Care Home, when the nurses were taking the remains of Suzy as directed by her physician through the back door and from the view of other patients, she was the next to arrive in a dark black American model Escalade with a six-thousand engine horsepower and in the company of three other persons. The car stopped on the driveways as its occupants stayed put for close to five minutes talking to each other before stepping out without the fourth person in the back seat. Led by a grey-haired man who after entering introduced himself as the escort nurse from the London Metropolitan Hospital with personal identification number RN 12670 produced a medical history and social status about the patient in the car. The Insurer or payee to every bill of the patients also introduced himself as Desmond Jotter and asked for the Standard Operation Procedure (SOP) of the facility which was readily produced making him take a seat only to start reading from point to point. The head of the facility looked through the medical short notes and smiled adding at least this one is not sick just old and weak. With the inspections done, records well read, and facility inspected, two men walked the old, frayed, and weak woman whose countenance says a lot about herself as the receiving nurse pitied her as her bags and baggage were carried away in good order until she sat down and looked around.

So; tell me where is this place? She began... well before the answer arrived, she looked at the facility manager only to as if she is just a wayside nurse working for money or a regis-tered nurse with full experience...

Well, there you have it, one of the transferring nurses said in a low tone, she is weak but her intelligence and accuracy of speech is very alive and alert most of the time. Know how not to underrate her, he added and walked out after documentation was complete and signed by both parties. Nancy who was part of those who wheeled her to the corner reached out to her medical history and began to read as follows;

Name; Hello White
Sex; Female
Initial visiting date; 17th June 2005
Birth Date; 9th September 1935
Address; 12A Silver Lane East London Road
SWN 3
Digital Location; 0.00123 5340987
Occupation History; Political Correspondent
(Investigative Journalist)
Condition; weak muscular joints with painless
swellings around her knees
Blood Group; B+
Very emotional to emotion swing from point to
point making her talk repeatedly and can really
vide into a verbal verbose. Mostly about so
many issues over nothing at all. A fragile
woman with sharp intellect and quick
tempered; please handle with care.
Signed Physician…

Well, well, well; Nancy sounded after reading what is on the medical form. Miss Hello White. And who are you she responded to Nancy with a sharp look. Have you ever respected before? Come on, you; slim face woman and a poor kind of nurse.

Do you have an elderly in your home at all, and if so; why not grant me a pinch of respect by adding Madam to my name? why can't you call me Miss if you can't say Madam Hello White... am older and by far wiser than you... am I talking or not? She questioned Nancy as other look on to what is happening. The raw and sudden exchange of the two parties become a testament to other nurse around as other patients were all unconcerned or their conditions prevented them from taking sides. Hello White is a retired political correspondent who served the British Broadcasting Corporation (BBC) for close to forty-five years with the first two years as an attaché, then three years as an intern before partial employment and the rest.

She served as Arabian news arena for close to ten years after served in Moscow, political bureau for seven years for during Soviet era and post-Soviet era. Her most rewarding location was Washington DC where she cemented her position with several insiders arresting, ambushing and making sure the BBC was the very first to broadcast political breaking news about American International Relation Policies around the world.

Her final five years was as an editor of political dialogues and was able to train ten new staff and four other judiciary news reporters raking in an amount of sixteen million pounce sterling as occupation benefits from benefactors, politicians, business builders and another close friend within high places of the food chain in Europe and America. Well, she has no children and as the only child of her parents, she has no heir to inherit her fortune of sixteen million pounce sterling with other fixed assets in Wales and Leeds.

Well, you Youngins (Youths or young adults) have over the years refused to read about ongoing issues only to read-meanings to every relationship aren't it huh? And how much will you pay me for my ideas and time? Old White requested as she keep her eyes to the moving pictures on the television screen. With both going silent, other nurse were looking on as if not interested but where possible would love to have a way to tame this patient like others are due to their health so that they can enjoy each other's company. Is one-hundred-dollar consultation fee oaky with you madam? Please listen up, you Youngins, my rate is two thousand and five hundred pounce sterling an hour for such duties, is either you pay or run-off and that is a fact. After that, she began to act silently and innocently as she looks at the ceiling of the room and the paintings on the wall as if looking to pick a point for a latter-day discussion. Ooh, I can see your toys, making others to toy around like children on steroids; tell me, is that a weapon to make them shut up huh? And with that said, no one answered and a sign that they are almost becoming feed up with her in less than twenty-four hours of stay. Will you Youngins answer me or not? She spoke out loud and the loudest answer she got was silence.

Then another nurse who did not experience what just went on showed up saying why is this place so quiet? Even Suzy's passing was well received... Ohhh, she is dead but by what means? Did she kill herself or you people help her go as it has done among your kind of profession? Hello questioned once again. Shut up you old witched of a kind... Mary yelled... the fact that you are rich and with political friends up the social ladder and the food chain does not mean you are the all-knowing kind of a bitch and if so then you are a witch? The old fool who can't control her mouth... she concluded.

There it is, a watercraft which is seven stories tall, with six levels of accommodation, two Christian churches, one Muslim mosque, one polyclinic, two roofed and fenced sports arena, a big dining hall, one hundred and seventy-seven cells out of which sixty for females, three hundred prison guards with twice their number in terms of guns, bullets and pepper spray, a computerized electric closing system, a kitchen which can feed six hundred men three square meals per day, two visitors holding area, one well-stocked library with seven thousand books, and no cable television allowed no matter what. It's a floating barge and that is where some call home as they are locked up behind bars which is commonly called State prison. The floating barge is one hundred and eighty-two meters long and fifty-seven meters wide in width house constructed from metals, fiberglass, and other durable and bulletproof materials from all parts of the world. There are five hundred female prisoners and five thousand two hundred and ten males locked behind bars and from that number are three thousand Youngins between the ages of eighteen and twenty-four years old serving a total of seven hundred and eleven combined years over decisions made during anger and poor thinking.

You see, the Venison base correction center near New York is a big boat just that it hardly moves about as it has been tied to the harbor and its accommodation system has one of the poorest ventilation systems in the United States of America and for its inmates, a wild boat which has refused to sail the oceans of the world. Thirty years ago, when such a facility was proposed, several prisoners or yet-to-be inmates were thinking that; it will be a kind of place to jump off easily but then they were wrong, and the only inmate who tried to escape just because the place sucks was easily fished out by several policemen patrolling in high-speed boats on the surface of the waters for re-entry. And that is where Tracy showed up that evening when she entered the metaverse. That day was a Sunday morning when she entered the hall which serves as the church for all females and all were seated in a sudden religious manner which had it not been they behind bars, would never have happened.

In their orange state-accepted cloths like shipyard or dry-dock workers' uniforms all were busy talking to each other is a sort of click except one Youngins who saw her and was very ill in spirits only to yell who are you little fool? Making the others to turn their heads in a surprise to see a new inmate but in a clean and different attire all altogether. Pooh-pooh, I know that bitch; a fanny-speaking lady from the front said to the others but even so, two hairless inmates walked up to Tracy and asked so what's your Nikki? Without a word, another showed up at her back only to pull her by her hair and talk at the top of her voice, she is a witch, she is a witch sent to spy on us all, even ye girls!! A wild frenzy response was coming from all as even in a chapel a wild fighting ensued, a sort of free-for-all open war in which any girl or woman grabs any close by to start the punching of face, pulling the hair, and throwing things about including the holy scripture which serves as the word of God. Tracy was under as three other women were fighting on top of her body hurting and even a lone woman trying to pull her out but is it an act to help or is her fighting partner she was looking for? Another reached for her fine clothes only to tore part of it and kept pulling as she lay beneath the huge body of people and almost becoming naked and the only thing that she could say was help-me, please help me, please help me...

And they fought a sort of free for all fight such that; when the prison pastor showed up to preach, blood was seen on the faces of some, front teeth were removed, several human hairs were seen flying around with six women in severe pain as they lay on the floor. And her gentle female voice tone could not do any good except a gunshot into the side walls of the structure by a no-nonsense prison officer; who has ever killed an inmate before out of anger and nothing happened to his position, his salary or his stay in the prison service and not even a letter of warning from the top Officer and they all know him so well. If you joke with Officer Daniel Jimmy Fokker, he will fuck you off with his loaded gun and that is a fact people. And then she was taken away into the officer's inn, a holding area reserved for only officers for questioning and how she managed to enter such a dangerous place reserved for a selected few.

After some hours of no really interested, Hannah visited the meta only to appear in the wide and open tall grass landscape where to her right is an upland almost resembling a table overlooking the open ocean. Well, is this Southern part of Africa or some other place? A well-built and muscular dark complexion young man suddenly appeared only to introduce himself as Dingo from the Province of KwaZulu Natal in South Africa. Well, please walk with me... Dingo said, adding I will be your guard and personal helper here, as there are several roaming predators from lions, Kruger, leopard, hyenas, cheetah and even snakes lurking in the tall grass. Come on, follow me please... they began to walk in a steady pace in the cooling sunshine as the sun dick gently slides behind them and down the skies. They walked for close to ten minutes only to come across a small village built whose individual clay house are arranged to form a circular set up with one entrance. And with the cool prevailing air across the Table Mountain, the children began to gather around the naked fire set by the old woman whose facial wrinkles talks of her struggles in life, hardship, pains of child birth and years of experience across the great wide plains. Well, if not mistaken, she will be close to a century in age and in wisdom. Mama Zimba, the old grey short hair woman with dime eye sight began to tell some selected stories to the growing number of children some of which are her biological grandchildren, all cloth below and any can say they were half naked yet very happy about their lives with several things yet to explore.

Mama Zimba began her story by saying... In the beginning were some selected tribes from Ashanti, Bantu, Ewe, Egypt, Fulani, Hausa and even the strong Zulu foraging, hunting and gathering and sleeping rough upon the land. But as it is in the vast ocean where the small fish eats the tiny fish, and small fish being eaten by the big fish and finally the big fish being eaten by a bigger fish, so was the unwritten terms and conditions across the wild part of the land. In the process of time; two leading tribes emerged being bigger and organized to face the test of time. One is the tribe which fights, conquers, rule by force and oppression, burning down opponent or loosing tribal land and property, raping their women by force after killing all children below the ages of ten years including young girls to make the captured women ready for childbirth within the possible time. With force all weak people flees and the brave ones submit by the will of their spears, sharp knives and poisonous arrows. To them life is war and he who masters the art of war is enforce the will of the gods of the land.

The other is the tribe which capture by a stratagem, adsorbs new ideas and tactics, secret combinations, play the indirect rule game, control the people by wooing their women and damsels, encourages the people to maintain their original language, festivals and rituals without burning down opponent property, making their women warm their beds at night at their own will and choice but tasking the conquered men to work hard in chains after selling off young boys leaving the damsel who offer to nay tribal soldier who needs her for marriage; by so doing are the originators of polygamy upon the continent of Africa. With weird rules, weak people flee and the brave once submit by inner faith that someday all shall pass; at least is better to be alive than to be killed by their bloody swards. To them life is as you see it, it's either a make or break and whichever way the gods of the land will have no say at all.

When to eat, what to eat, and how to eat are all the very common and known ways which every master tells his slave to do, and what even saddens me is the free women doing nothing to support the impoverished and ill-treated slave girls and women around their homes compared to the free men who may offer their fellow men slave water to drink during a hard day's work even if it's not enough or it's unclean water, oh what a shame on the part of the free women... then comes the two common ways of a poor slave girl who have never made an attempt to run away but with such an act, is it an act of loyalty? Or an absolute African Juju or Voodoo or again an African dark spell cast upon them?

The men carry heavy loads on their heads to far distant villages and cottages in the vast green forest on empty stomachs for hours. In a forest town governed by a willful Chief, when a male slave is accused of seeing the nakedness of a Slave-Master's daughter, he is stripped naked and given thirty-six strokes on his back and after chained openly for seven days without food except water which is smuggled at night by fellow male slave to serve him. Polygamy is an accepted practice for freemen and as they like; as others willingly view the nakedness of slave women to entertain themselves but not for a male slave; as such an act of even seeing the nakedness of a free woman if even a girl is a crime punishable by an unwritten law of the village.

The unwritten law of the War Lord of Anlong (Anlo) an Ewe Ruler. To every slave is another slave whose treatment is odd, sad, and painful like a toothache but who is to care for such a slave? The slave master rules both the human spirit and body of their slave such that a slave is but a devotee and the master is but a god whom the sun never sets.

The Slave Master seek bodily comfort from the young damsels ignoring the older women sometimes and not only them but their young women in their teenage periods and exploits them for fun and pleasure. Again, some men wanting to know how potent they are or men being accused of being the cause of their childless marriages or condemned as impotent try their manhood on the poor slave girls to prove a point especially when the slave girls become pregnant.

Is on this note that the War Lord began to pick and seize such slave girls from their owners and who are you to complain against the War Lord of Anlong or the Ewe Ruler? The pregnant slave has no day off, no weekends, no vacation, and is even made to work with her poor health conditions without any support even during the festival period which all are given rest upon the land but not such a group of slaves. Hence, the laws of the War Lord are but three;

1. Any pregnant and ill-treated slave is taken or seized by the War Lord.
2. The offspring of such slaves becomes the property of the house of the War Lord offering service till the end of their lives with the males serving as soldiers in the warriors tracking army.
3. Any free man wanting such girls who have become a woman for marriage shall consult the elders of the War Lord; and after paying a token can then take her to wife, as a concubine, or as a house help but not as a slave anymore.

A small female voice which sounded like one missing an octave began to sing a native song and in less than a minute all others joined the singing making those almost dozing to be alert to the proceedings of the moment... the song lasted for almost two short minutes; after which the story began again...

The Common Act of the Occupant of the Golden Throne, King of Ashanti. To every slave is another slave whose treatment is hell, strange, and with some calling for the spirit of death who seems to be far, far away from them. They call Death per season but Death has ears that can't hear their call, Death has eyes but can't see or is short-sighted, Death has servants serving him with information on earth per second but it looks like they are acting lazy and poorly located to grant their cry. The half-naked slave girls scrub the backs of the sick, weak, and old men and women of their master, cook their meals, and clean their rooms all in the early hours of the morning before their main task on the farm.

The masters seek bodily comfort from the young damsels forgetting the women sometimes and not only them but their young male family members men exploiting them for fun and pleasure. Again, some forest men wanting to know how potent their herbal medicines can be on their manhood results; as men whose wives are on long distant journeys reach out to the slave girls, any pregnancy is never counted as theirs in any way and their wives are never alarmed too over such acts. For years past till now; women have never helped the course of their fellow women in any way.

In this way, the Occupant of the Golden Throne began to act. The pregnant slave irrespective of where she was, was seized, picked from, or bought and had no say at all. And the laws are but three also;

1. Any pregnant and ill-treated slave is taken or seized by the Occupant for a season. The owner is fined a goat and two fowls payable to the palace fine collector within a week.
2. After one hundred and fifty days of childbirth, the poor slave returns to her owner to serve, as the child is given to the palace team of older women to raise the baby to childhood.
3. The offspring of such slave becomes the property of the Occupant of the Golden Throne offering service till the end of their lives with the males serving as part of the palace security team.

Meanwhile at the same period in another country well across the territorial boundaries of eastern Europe and below Russia was a young male in his early twenties, a handsome man belonging to a rich and popular family, in fact; a royal by an Arabian standard stepped into the well-decorated living room with full of golden ornaments and sat in one of the choice sofas. Rahman Abdul Saudi reached for the gold-plated ocular quest device after unplugging it from the charging setup and wearing it. He sat in the comfort and privacy of his ancestral royal home as within seconds surfaced in the northern arctic coast of Russia. As a Youngins, she paid up a sum of one thousand and eighty hundred meta-cedis only to get to that far as money is never a problem to such an individual.

In the lower level or degree of the Meta, it looks like being in the uncompleted building or what Americans will say the projects and downtowns of a locality, and any in there can never visit the second or third level without certification or security clearance. All those in the second degree or level can visit the lower degree but not the higher degree. It's only the third-degree or higher-level certified people who can visit the second and lower-degree without any prior notice. The prisoners, odd and wild people, murderers, rapists, corrupt officials, and any slapped with fines and tags to be punished are all grouped and confined in the lower degree of the meta until they have done their time as stipulated and interviewed by the Meta-Zone officials. As soon as Rahman Abdul Saudi entered the meta, he activated the Virtual Intersection Protons Screen popularly called (VIPS); with Vips, he entered the Russian Northern Fleet Military warehouse where he saw everything and nobody saw or noticed his presence; he walked toward the sealed-up object partly covered with a black rubber cloth as it sits silently at the left corner of the dry floor. Wishing to pull off the rubber but did not as any who is very observant will know something has gone wrong. The big warm room was partly dark but with the help of his flashlight walked over to the left corner where he saw an electronic medium-range weapon system under construction, by the side was written St Petersburg Polytechnic, Department of Electronics Research item.

He took pictures and sent them over to his Google Cloud account, the dark and warm room encouraged him further as after all, no one knew he was in there and besides that, he was under the intelligence of the Vips; he jumped a shell of a bomb only to walk down the stairs to another level of the holding area. The Youngins switched on the lights only for a sea of Military hardware to lay before his Arabian eyes, from electronics, unfused bombs of all types, radar jammers, stingers, surface-to-air rockers and air to surface rockers and all in a perfect array and arrangement as if about to be shipped to an African country to start a war. The strong room which is about two hundred and fifty meters by eighty meters long and a height of fifty meters is build out of metallic pools and aluminum sheets. It is air tight with dry floors and a small room for quick human access. The big gate is electric operated and with ears close to the walls, any can feel the vibrations of vehicles moving in the outside yard. With the lights on, the Youngins took more than twenty and two perfect pictures where with some, he removed the covering cloths before taking them.

In attempt to take a particular picture, he stepped on a lose rope which dropped on to the floor and in so doing made a cylindrical metal rod to fall from a height of about two meters which made a loud metallic sound but that wall all until it happened. A small door on the metallic door suddenly pushed into the room only for two Russian uniform men to step into the room and after looking round saw nothing and thinking of going away but another military official with the name tag Vinovich walked over and with flash lights ordered them to find and see what caused the sudden metallic sound. The men walked into the room, very worried about the order but have no choice as it's an order and not a suggestion, began walking around from lane to lane and almost reaching the very location of the Youngins who as at now is hidden under a Russian tanker; they soon saw what caused the sound and reported as required and walked out of the hard ware facility. Rahman; very terrified, body energy sipping fast, sweating even in an ice-cold country and nearer to the north pole, he soon recovered after almost two minutes of hiding and began to walk silently as there may be security dogs sniffing all over. He walked silently till after passing close to ten armed tanks, fifteen medium size hoover crafts, twenty-two speed boats with turbo engines and ten sonar detectors all in their boxes or cases.

After the first curve left, then the second right; only to see a well written alert or information or even warming written boldly in red-paint or ink on the wall. And when he stopped, he mastered courage and walked six steps closer only to see a small digital keys with figures or numbers from zero to nine, signifying all or any who want to cross from that point must know they key numbers or key combinations. Not knowing what to do and even so, wanting to see what lies within the other side, he began to think hard and at the edge wanting to take the risk. He moved his right hand

and gradually pointed his index finger to the first digits being zero and pressed it twice. With that done the small green screen produced two sets of words EN, RU, CN, and FH which stand for English, Russian, Chinese, and French respectively. So, he selected EN (English) and the screen produced the systematic lay which he memorized after reading and was a bit lucky on.

He pressed; the sixteen key combination which was (0182673986528046) and entered... the electric soft close gate began to slide to the lefthand side and gradually the whole place was as open as the Arabian sky free from the sand storm only for him to see what lies in there all by himself. In the similitude of the Olympic swimming pool, the protected water hole began to open on its secret and what lies in there. The Olympic-sized pool was partly frozen, transparent, and crystal clear like the Caspian Sea in its early frozen period as a yellowish block of regular objects was scattered below and almost half full. Fearing it may be electrified, Rahman did not even try to dip his finger into the pool instead reached out for a rod and cast it into the pool hoping something would happen but nothing went wrong. Again, he looked around to make a small basket from some wire mesh and managed to remove one of the blocks of the yellowish metal only to see, feel, and smell it with a firm conclusion that it was a bar of gold. But what will solid gold be doing in a military hardware or weapon storage facility huh?...

Does gold take sides in wars? Does wars feed and run on pure solid gold or what? Or perhaps it's the prized trophy of the war, the winner takes it away.

Not willing to pocket any of the pure gold which is purer than what his fellow royals have in their hold, Rahman was very surprised over just that item and smiled with much wonder of thought. The Russian Northern Naval base which houses the North Air-Craft Carriers for war, Nuclear Submarines, other frigates, mine sweepers, combined attackers, Cruisers, and other deep sonar military research ships were all in the ice harbor as the large naval seamen were in a state of relief which is once per year in a mariner's life. Still not trusting the Russians and thinking the swimming pool was electrified, he walked out of the room only to enter another close to the general public facility which served as the main area where Stalin ordered several scientific experiments with some being the use of life human beings as Guinea pigs during the cold war era with the United State of America. Well, today that is not allowed but what they did then has given birth to some scientific advances to the human anatomy which is now used in the area of Vaccines, the immune system, and heart medicines.

Like an African gorilla on a rampage just to protect its territory, the smallish Youngins walked out from the room and pressed the keys in any other for which by so doing the electric door dropped halfway and stopped. He took to his left-hand side walking for about twelve meters only to discover other stirs leading to a hidden basement after a minute stop, he drew closer and kept walking only to see a sharp bend where a cold subterranean tunnel well-lit with lights leading to somewhere best known to those who built it. He began walking knowing his Vips would do the work but then after halfway heard some voices drawing closer to him and no matter his speed it would be impossible to escape from them, before he could say a word, he saw a Russian Naval officer with full honors well flanked by two naval sea men two steps after him as they advance towards him. Very terrified, so bitter, afraid, and almost passing out as there is nowhere to hide. Twelve meters, ten meters, four meters, five steps then two steps till the uniform men walked past him as if he is a wallpaper on the walls of the tunnel which needs no regards. Rahman was very shocked only to feel so silly as he looked at them walk away. Now acting a bit like Charlie Chaplain, he could not believe what just happened as he kept on looking, he later sat on the floor and began to smile and now believes the Vips works and he will be the living testimony of the Western electronic miracle. He kept aiming at the direction he was heading towards and in no time, the end was in sight as four uniformed men tow at each side were detailed to keep the way clear from intruders even from within. With his pointers, he later checks out of the Russian facility where should he want to go back; will have to pay as he did earlier, and it's true that money talks.

Day in and day out all get busy with the meta maintaining a constant act and becoming a faithful devotee as Hello, the most constant critic looks on with no show of her own. Then comes one day when after a long talk aimed at no particular person within the facility, Hannah went closer, and spoke to her about the Ocular Quest VR and what anybody can achieve, can be, and can do on the meta making her look on with open eyes. Hannah decided to tolerate her for a season by helping her put on the Ocular quest for the very first time and lo, and behold she surfaced at a big, warm, and empty hall where world leaders all over the world meet to discuss world politics, development and even talk about war games and even threaten each other where possible. And that hall is the United Nations General Assembly Hall in New York.

Then she sat down, crossed her legs only to pull out her book and pen as if about to make short-hand notes. A set of lights were turned off only for new once to come on and it was there that she knew she wasn't alone in there, strangely it looks like there is somebody in helm of affairs with the lights. A smallish man in white long sleeves surfaced and without asking any question began to open the treated Lebanon red and wide wood door as in less than five minutes; well clothes men in a black and brown office suit representing their governments began to fill the circular seat in the form of the letter cee "C". Yes, the saw her seated with pen and paper and thinking she was a UN staff did nothing to let her walk out. The all-men club began to talk free, wild and coded as words like red-hot, willing strikes and killing factors was all over. The Russian ambassador to the UN accused Britain and France of trying to poison the atmosphere with sanctions as after their remarks all other person began to shift the conversation all in favor of the wild Syrian President still holding on to political power. He added, Moscow will activate his killing factor over any who dare enters the special zone reserved for children and women, we will rain bombs over all irrespective of who is on the ground just try it... he added. The meeting of ambassadors, from United States of America, China, Britain, France Russia, Canada, Egypt and Nigeria did not like such a rash and hash comment from a willing country but then, all he wanted was what he said. Feeling bad and wanting to talk as a journalist, Hello in a shocking move which is never allowed in the security council meeting raised her hands just to draw their attention for which some did see it but ignored her little hand and went on with the meeting of talking hard. And when the issue of Yemen popped up, she stood up wanting to say something as she began by saying... I have been to Yemen and what I saw is... the assistant American ambassador yelled shut up you little and small mind kind of a person; by the way who invited you here huh? You better sit down ...was the last order; making her fall back to her seat like a stone fallen from the sky. The all-men club was not willful in words but in deeds and not even the United Nation high officials or top staff can order them around in the building like they do to Poor African and Asian countries representatives, these are the big boys and the movers and shakers of the global order of commence aiming to form a new world order.

Hello was silenced sharply, worried, with sick inner spirit if not killed, as tears stream down her smooth left cheeks remembering what was going on in the war afflicted Yemen as what is being discussed is far from what is happening on the ground level of the country with refuges number millions going hungry, sick with several children dying per each passing day; the planed and well reported humanitarian relief items does not get to the intended person but ends up in the hands of the soldiers who consumes them and with some using theirs to bargain for sex from the small and available young girls and women resulting in unsafe abortions all over the dry countryside. An "SF "activity which means, Sex for Food, kills the Islamic faith which most people once owned as the true way.

When the three hours meetings ended, they smiled, shook hands as the so-called fuming men stuck their files under their armpits after picking up all that belonged to them from the table rendering it clean, shook hands with their opponents across the divide as if nothing went on as they enter the very next hall for lunch. And with they doing all this, the real problem about the war in Yemen wasn't discussed, and that of Syria too. And these all-boys club will take their pay from their governments as per plan. With all gone away, with several things discussed about nothing at all; Hello went silent only to say... So, God are you there? Did you see and listen to these men talk? And what are you doing about all these solvable issues of the world; yet men in political suits have no plans to do just that as your children die in the name of talks, some raped for food... what is wrong with this world groomed and controlled by the all-men club with no fear of the universal law? She got so close to power but failed to do her duty in favor of those children and pitiful women of Syria and Yemen. And when the lights began to go off, she left the meta only to surface as a changed old woman, so silent that all the other nurses were asking each other what did she see in the Meta? Did she visit the Jurassic Park animals who chased her off or the African Zoo?

Hannah asked "is everything ok? For which she answered yes and thank you.

But is it possible that; he who has a bad behavior in on earth would exhibits bad behaviors in the Meta? Tracy began...

If you are good, you will certainly be good in the meta, if you are a racist, nothing will change over your character in the meta. Even any lazy person either man or woman will continue to be lazy still and nothing can change it except himself. May began by saying... "The very spirits which possessed you during your period here on earth, it is the same spirits which will possess you in the meta; so, what is the point here... Margaret asked? When we act as mere mortals without reasoning, we are but animals in the wild hence all must act and not to be acted upon as in schooling his mind and calibrating his attitude which is a needed recipe to make one a good citizen of the meta. When you come across a hooligan in the meta, such a person is a hooligan in the real life and likewise a rapist, a womanizer, a robber and corrupt officials.

What about they who are mentally odd or mentally ill huh? I have no idea about that, Tracy began but; may I state that, a crazy person or mentally ill person would not have the audacity to put on the meta with the ability to do as needed and even should that happen, he or she will be as he was in the real world and may not enjoy or take note of whatever he comes across. But, but... what about politicians? Are you trying to say that the president of United States of American who rules and control the country will still be the president in the meta world huh, come on talk to me? I bet to differ Miss...

As a president, he controls but on the meta he is but nobody, can be attacked and he can also attack for the constitution does not extends it long hands there and to my knowledge that is a fact. Well, you have a point Tracy finally accepted without further comment. The silent body of the great robber which has not yet been discovered still lies in his bed as the registered nurse's gist and chats over what was experienced during the meta events which is still on commercial break. Mr. Tony Wood was loved as his illness made him speechless and all his raw and rough language as a robber and killer has either been erased from his mind or can't be expressed verbally. He lay with about six hundred and fifty health found to his name and with no direct or known family members, only God knows what will become of that money. His may be buried as soon as possible, by people he barely knows and if not cremated in the central crematorium owned by the city of London, then it will be that of the town folks. The old and fray man even in death is far richer compared to several walking people on the street of London and even the very nurses caring for him.

Twenty-two years ago, two immigrants from one of the Southeast Asian countries were granted passage only to surface in London where the man, Mr. Joko Kong gained employment as an airport airside cleaner as his wife Marah also got a cleaning appointment in one of the local private schools. In less than two years, they saw the arrival of a baby boy who was named Jack Koh Kong and that marked their family history in the city of London and Britain. The baby boy grew so fast and so loved that; as the only son and child, end up becoming a spoiled fellow as his troubled teenage days made him end up in detention for twelve days. Jack Koh Kong who soon became Kojak landed in jail to serve twelve years after attempting a bank robbery which failed, as two of the ring members were killed by the London terrorist police. Kojak's parent were so sorry for what their son had become that his mother died out of depression followed by the father in just seven months. Kojak was not given the privilege to be at their funerals and burial site. In his early seventies, the very morning which Tony Wood the unknow and unforeseen bank robber passed on, Kojak was the very person to replace him and to also occupy the same room and bed.

He was picked to belong to that very facility due to the fund reserved and invested for him by his late parents some thirty-seven years back which he did not know until a half-burnt document in his late father's files said so. Without a job, a place to lay his head and money, he slept rough till was one day knocked down by a drunken driver on the side street of Abbey Avenue where the onlooking public sent him to the hospital. He spent six hours at the general hospital after initial two head surgeries and lower lips stitching which prevented him from opening his mouth hence, avoided solid food for the past five and half months. And when he arrived, and when he showed up; the first two nurses who cast an eye on him nearly went back as the third nurse took two steps back for real. His head was unusual and not from birth but as a result of vehicular accident, as the perfect word to use that; is lack of a better word is an irregular shape yet he is still breathing. He had just one seeing eye, one ear, a partly touched or constructed nose using skin from other parts of his body, a deformed forehead and a soft hanging cheek skin or cheek flesh which has been under the medical knife for four times with each period of working lasting for four hours of medical work and five weeks to recover. His daily makeup work as directed by the department of Burns and Facial Reconstruction was quite effective but even so; after all that work if even done for him by a make-up artist, the whole thing looks like a cosmetic surgery gone too far, his good mood smiles even when looks like a chimpanzee at will. Kojak, now a retired public headache, now looks calm as his own age looks down upon him and with such a look, the best thing to do is to lay low and to keep a low profile.

He had his faculties at a score higher than most patient in there, fluent in French, English, German and Chinese the only person who can get close to him will be Miss Hello and that is all. With sharp intellects, speech and mathematical ability he may be a next new thing to do well in the meta. Kojak, the British Thai settled down not getting worried about how others look at him and at least hopeful that he now has a place to put his head, a team of care givers to care for his needs and after all his father loved him despite all that he put him through in life. Just as he arrived, Tony Wood was taken out and through a back door as the mortuary staff arrived to take him away and without establishment about his family and social friends, his body will be kept for just seven months only for his biological data taken and added to the growing number of unclaimed bodies and buried in a large open and later unmarked grave about sixty miles from the city of London.

Meanwhile; there is a big rally going on in central London, a protest over the legalization of gay and its full rights under the daylight of the sun as given to all mortals on earth. The street on the Meta was filling part as several people from all walks of life who looked forward to such propositions and even onlookers rushed or logged on to see how things are going on the Meta. With the meat, should a rally, protest, or civil walk in any part of the world... there would be more than a million-million people who will not ask for traveling visas, airline tickets, and booking of accommodation to attend such events on the meta.

The Arabian Youngins were there, African healthy folks and other European supporters including football hooligans were all set into positions for effective rally or protests. The world of gay has almost become that which is owned by the Youngins form several countries of the world who don't need the permission of their parents to attend.

FISH BONE

Something must kill a man... something must kill a man... something must kill a man he finally said whilst sitting by the table well displayed with a whole range of alcoholic beverages.

Well, meet John Cool one of the seasoned investigative British journalists born in York to Mr. Alex James Cool and Madam Cynthia Forson all of whom are of blessed memory some twelve years back. He lives in the meta, dines in the meta, acts with the meta and finally lives for the wellbeing of the meta, in fact you can confidently say he is a resident journalist in the meta. At age eleven years, he lost interest in school and easily became a school dropout moving from point to point in the York market with parent unaware till an open school football games where anybody is permitted to participate called for his attention. He joined an open team of other stray and way ward boys too play against John Bolton primary where he scored the only goal of the match and was easily noticed and picked out to join the school's team after the game which by so doing, he gains his interest for school through sports and completed primary school only to be awarded a sport scholarship for the Junior secondary which he accepted without letting his parents know. Today he is a trained journalist from London school of journalism yet sit by the table of alcohol doing what huh?

By the way what is the purpose of drinking alcohol? What is the real purpose of drinking an alcohol? Is it not to get drunk?? If so, why drink an expensive alcohol like Hennessy, Vodka, Scottish dry gin, Bacardi Cloud nine, Amarula, Alomo Bitters if you can equally drink any cheap drink on the market and get drank... or why do people get drank expensively? With his heavy eyes coupled with poor vision, slow and deep voice tone and too heavy to move his body from the chair he is sitting, he began to construct these words all by himself;

The Art of Drinking

1. Know where to locate the alcohol
2. The origin of the alcohol
3. The percentage of the alcohol
4. Define the tort or volume to consume
5. Check the after tase effect
6. The feeling in the drink
7. The stream of drunkenness or confidence level

What is wrong with the United Nation at all, what is wrong with its head or the occupants of various positions such that they can't arrest the ever-growing challenges of this world? From Africa, Asian, South America and the middles east... it looks like is Europe and America is okay then all is well isn't it, people? Truth be told, truth really get told these days... The United Nation is drinking an expensive alcohol and does not know that, every alcohol can get you drank? The United Nation regulations regulates all but favors others and leaves the rest in the dark. Ooh, getting drank expensively...

John Cool meets Hello White, the slim tall young lady in her late twenties walked past the middle-aged man drinking his soul out but her sharp eye saw the laminated card around his chest indicating that he is a member of a press but which media house and why the early morning parade of alcohol as if that is the only breakfast on the meta... She stopped and walk up to him only to ask, please where is the nearest eatery down here Sir? Okay, who are you and what is your sole purpose in this world reserved for men only? Okay, don't worry, walk ahead and after twenty meters take left and stop at a pink and white painted stand, that is where food is cooked. He added... okay and she walked away. She did ad per told only to arrive at a perfumery shop but instead of getting angry, she made friend with the woman who helped her out and that was that, she later surfaced at the Orient Hall in the United Nation banquet hall that same day only to see the same self-made drinking man in his best of clothes and ready to bit hard at any world leader and other diplomates who dare saw up for lunch. Hello introduced herself only for Cool to accept seeing hers that morning as it looks like the alcohol did not do much damage to his sense of recognition. Well, my name is Hello White and a retired journalist for the British Broadcasting Corporation but currently a freelance Journalist within the meta. Well come to the family Mr. Cool said to assure her ability. My name is John Cool and worked for the Aljazeera News in Doha but most hopping from the continent of Africa to Asia and twice in Central Europe. How long have you been community of the United Nation? Hello asked... Well just sixteen and half sad years... was the responds. Sixteen and half sad years huh? What made your stay here sad and have you detected the cause of the sadness and even how come you are still here?

For the past sixteen and half years, I have come across close to five hundred and twenty diplomats all from several countries around the world with good personal achievements which is so rich that; it looks like there is nothing which they can't work on. Again, have seen close to one thousand United Nation staffs which the best of clothes and uniforms which money can buy, rich academic achievements, with thousands of acquittances and contacts from both home country and abroad, to rely on for help yet what did they do? I have been so close to death, seen death and have been visited by death on several evidence finding or facts finding missions in Western Asia, The Middle East regions, Eastern Europe, Southern America and Northern parts of Africa which upon the risk, after our submissions all were swept under the diplomatic carpets of the United Nations by individuals representing powerful countries I don't want to mention as at now and soon you will know them too by yourself.

The preps for those countries say what they want or being asked to say by downplaying what we have worked for from the jungles of war, the truths of wars are tossed to the diplomatic dogs of the day, why such an act? Are we all not humans, are the Asian more humans than Africans? Are Arabians not humans too or are the south Americans not humans too? So; what is the point by paying attention to some details and turning a blind eye to the rest? The United Nation is behaving like as if it knows all things, can do all things and in fact, he is in the comfortable lead of issue over events on the ground across the world by waiting too long to attempt to solve it. If you think am wrong, just google it...... after the rejection, the very same people are seen at lunch satisfying themselves with good food and fine wines, if the United Nation is drinking heavily and any kind of alcohol can get you drank then; I personally think the United Nation is getting drank expensively...... And what is the point huh? Soon after the effects of the alcohol is gone, it will need an Indian painkiller called Dolo to ease the headache.

By that time the Russians would be busy checking their grades, Americans cross-checking their money from the spoils of war as the poor Africans and others from the third-world countries looking up for results but will get nothing, as their women and children curse the very day they were conceived. At times the United Nations wants to buy time before rushing to solve a pressing problem and can easily predict who did that; but why buy time when there is none on sale?

I have been in the Meta, live for the Meta, and am a resident within the Meta but have nothing to point my fingers at; that it's the United Nation that stopped this war or that war... Or it's the United Nation that silenced America, tamed Russia, woo France and diplomatically asked Britain to avoid the verbose and asked China to keep his long-stretched hands to himself. Syria is still cooking; Yemen is burning as African Libya has collapsed. The middle and central European countries are still under the shadow of he who I rarely mention these days. Why all these huh? Isn't it better to build people or a team by lighting a fire within them compared to lighting a fire beneath them? Which is which? The United Nations general working staff are pretending to be working as their employer pretending to be paying. The regions of North Sudan, Congo, Northern Nigeria, Chad, Mali, Ukraine, Colombia, and Myanmar, are all not yet free from the woods of war and terrorist activities. These are the regions where politicians stay rich by living like they are poor when the United Nations diplomats show up, as there are more problems at the doors of the United Nations compared to solutions and chances are that those solutions would never be implemented unless those permanent countries say so. By the way any questions huh? Cool asked back after raining volumes of problems over the years. Ahh, so where do I start my work from or which of the affiliates can be of good use? Is it the American or Russian diplomats for attention, what about the Chinese diplomats?

On the other side of things; the United Nations is just like the biggest fish market in Accra which is the capital of Ghana and equally the fish market with the widest variety of species of fish from smoked fish, dried fish, fresh fish, oil fried fish, salted fish, cooked fish and even dry powder fish used in the meals for children and people recovering from poor health at the hospitals.

Go out there and do something for God and country, go out there and do something for the venerable few of the world, don't cash after money and just be with them but don't be like them. John Cool with his eyes peeled looked keenly into the eyes of Miss Hello like lovers trying not to end their relationship, and after all that was said, Hello smiled and walked away knowing in about ten minutes, the Close Door meeting of representatives on nuclear weapons will be in-seating which she as a freelance journalist cleared by the United Nations is permitted to be an observer. And when it started, she looked at them trying to work out the relative ages of those men without a single woman to lighten up the meeting or is it that men are more inclined towards mathematics and physics or what at all is the problem here? Again, she kept her eye peeled, her brain sparking several pieces of information to quantify the ages of the all-men meeting supposed to last just forty-five minutes, will they be Youngins or non-Youngins? At the head of the table is Dr. Cad-Brown the Physicist from Britain, Dr. Zelensky from Russia, Professor Pudor from France, Dr. Xi Zeng from the People's Republic of China, Professor Loadstone from the United States of America and Dr. Adolf Yankovic from Russia but United Nation staff well vexed in quantum mathematics. Well, they soon began without a prayer like most religious groups of the world do, no political anthem and no patriotic pledge except a handshake which had it not been a United Nations rule it would never come to pass. The table of men sometimes called the Rivalry arena, they began working out the number of total nuclear war head of every nation which none there gave, none there approved off, but was gotten by prediction of physicist and nuclear chemist working as consultants for the United Nations some twenty-five years ago and is updated every seven years. France total war head was peg at the mid hundreds, Britain at the far hundreds, China at the hundreds, United State at the hundreds and ten as Russia in the first thousand. For each representative, they did not nod their head to accept neither shock their heads in rejection as the United Nation staff give or run the numbers on the big screen displaying to all concerned.

So, the question to them all was; when will the increase of arms and nuclear weapon manufacture cease? Before France raised his hand to something, the whole room was fill with total silence as if the meeting is a silence meeting, the prep from France went like are you talking of reduction knowing Iran, Pakistan, Israel and others are also as deadly as we are? Have you thought of that huh? Don't say that, we better stop this meeting and go for lunch... was his last words. The rest did not utter a word making the forty-five minutes meet to end up in only ten minutes. In a bit of anger, Hello one of the observers questioned, so; is that all huh? Shut up and don't be silly... are you the one to tell us what to do and what not to do? One diplomat said out loud making other observers to creep into their shells as they remain seated. The Chinese representative stood up and went like who invited you here? You better mind your business else this will be the very last time at such a meeting. Well, with all seated and calm; the United Nation staff then went on with his presiding over the meeting by saying; without further information, discussions and any related questions, I push for the motion that this meeting has come to an end and will be called up when need. Thank you. The Russian then seconded the motion and that was all. Hello without any resentments over what happened was so sick that she branched off into the pharmacy section which is part of a small hospital within the United Nation building and called for painkillers and it was on this very medical counter when one of the participants representing America picked up his medications for an illness best known to him, is it that these men are medically sick and needs not to be at the helm of affairs? Or is it that all gathered in there are in hurry to do their personal stuff or were in hurry to walk away as they may be in pain and relief is what is really needed? Could hunger be the next thing on their minds as all were men? Humm, wonders will never end especially when an all-men meeting goes way ward. Are there not women within the United Nation general staff or can't the United Nation heads of departments or diplomats speak to these countries to bring in women?

With John Cool nowhere to be found to relate what just happened, Hello walked out after taking his pill and head towards the cafeteria for launch only to see two other representatives or nuclear diplomats of Britain and France in a company of other men all in sleek black suits one of which is a board member for an ammunition company based in France. And what is on sale and who is doing the buying? Hello began to think and talk to herself in her minds... this time despite those she met are part of those fit to be called Youngins, the power, the position and the personal wealth that each person holds are so huge that; they were able to shut her down and again she is just a guest and not a member of such meeting.

To every in-house patient, most couldn't hear what was going on, again others can hear but just do not care except for Hello and the Thai old man. They sang out loud and began to speak to each other as a small sharp kitchen knife began to go down the center of the cake for their eating pleasure. The wine of glasses began to kiss the tip of each other as for each kiss a glass-like cling sound is heard as several others were placed about fifteen meters from the forty-six inches flat-screen television to watch a family movie. Even the cooks, garden man, driver, and the three cleaners got their share of the cake making the small sideways part look like an end-of-year departmental party in honor of a litigant whom I wish not to say... after almost twenty-five minutes clear, a sudden phone call pulled the facility manager out from the many and the response of the phone call got the whole thing to go down as each head towards his or her unit or place of work.

So, the gravity of the phone is so big that it watered down your merry-making in just forty-five seconds... is that the case? Hello asked the very nurse who tried to push her off with her words and she could not answer as she walked away. That afternoon, Hello helped her hopes high knowing she would be having a visitor in the person of Jake Frost one of her past friends who walked along the corridors of diplomacy for close to forty years at the United Nations, and the American White House before his retirement which made him to relocate to Madagascar. It's he who once said; "Until the Lions have their own historian, the tale of the hunt will always go in favor of the hunter" the lanky and grey hair man in the company of two Youngins between the ages of twenty-seven and thirty-two years stopped in front of the care home and asked of the name and the reception which the security man did. The reception looked at him keenly when he asked of Hello White... that old and verbally ill woman huh? The receptionist said without fear or favor. When the two old birds saw themselves, they warmly embraced each other ignoring the health protocols which greets everybody who enters the facility, looked deep into each other's eyes and said, life is but the same everywhere... you look damn good girl; Jake Frost added. After sitting, they began their conversation from the rift and other issue concerning Israel and the Palestinian which to Jake, can one day spark a third world war.

Well listen to this, on the corridors of diplomacy, who courts who? Well, that is a straight forward answer but, in this century, it varies of other tail-tail issues especially when dealing with the so call super powers. But what is on your warm and cooking mind all these whiles? Hello asked... don't tell that, after all these while you still keep to writing pieces of articles for the New York times. Even around the circumference of wrings power no matter the location of the so-called power what must be-must be. So, who is courting who this time and for what at all? Hello requested form Jake.

If a master keeps lying and the message is always delivered by a particular messenger; then, there comes a time that if we want lairs, the messenger would be an extension of the lies too. Is that correct? Jake Frost demanded and hoping to get an answer from Hello. She went silent and blank for close to fifty-five seconds till Mr. Jake Frost cleared his throat to draw her attention. Okay, okay; I accept that proposition... she submitted her answer. Proposition you say; what kind of proposition is that? That is the truth and the whole truth... tell me what is eating you up man!!? You see, when the newly appointed United Nation humanitarian boss was appointed, little did he know that his room has been bugged. The Indian man is a forty-two years old man with partly burnt fingers, dry palms and with constantly dry face and well known for championing the world of Indian music, trade and agriculture in his home region. His first twenty-one days of communicating with top managers, office workers, drivers and even sweepers had all been recorded but by whom? And these recordings were found in the domain of the public, a total diplomatic break down of protocol making several cries to call for all staff within the United Nation to be sacked at once.

Give me a break she requested... So, what have you been doing all these whiles? Who have you been loving or who claimed love you when I wasn't around huh? You have aged like fine Spanish wine brewed two hundred years ago... come on say something my Dude... well, life hasn't been easy and of late have been taking good care of myself through the use of technology to do things, go places and access things from a distance and even if needed, travels less as needed. What about you Frost requested from Hello. I have been glued to this small place called home but feels more like a road side of dwelling with ladies with sharp lips to cast insults at you, should I have, my own way will escape to freedom but my personal health and motor nature have so slowed down such that, I need help to do all that in a smooth swipe. The two Youngins could not believe that, these old individuals are plotting an escape plan as even still despite so old loves themselves and began to wonder what is love at all that some can keep to it well while others so confused about it that their marriages have lasted just twenty-four hours after which are begging the law court for a bill of divorce, how right are they doing it?

In this young world where the Internet of things is but a must, I have been able to visit some strange places despite my knee problem and diabetic blood. Such places are the driest place on earth which is the western part of Chile, the most active oil rig in the Gulf of Mexico, and the Sulphur mines of Peru. Erhh, so; how did you embark on that journey from Africa as there is no direct flight? Hello asked...

You see, in this world of new technology, I have come across what is called the Internet of Things (IOT) where with technology, several things can be achieved in not attempting. One rich Youngins, the son of a local politician in an institute where I teach six hours per week introduced me to a new virtual device called Oculus Quest VR where and who has it can see into things, go places, and even be actively part of events at several places, do you believe that is possible huh? Yes, she responded... well, teaching, how good is that?

Well, forget about that, the most interesting thing is that electronic devices make it possible to dream or to make one dream come true for a season or a reason. Well, this Care Home has that too... Hello quickly pointed to it being plugged to power up the battery.

I had it on and in less than a minute was in a dry coastal desert land which has one of the lowest rainfall patterns in the world, and that is Chile. The high upland which lies so close to the open ocean has less rainfall or no rain at all making it so difficult to get hygienic water for use, out of every five people in that region, one and a half have no access to safe drinking water and as such poor crop production. But then the region is about two thousand meters above sea level and with high fog from the open ocean after several scientific works, a European Non-governmental company was able to devise a way to collect droplets of water from the passing fog which happens quickly and vanishes without saying bye. The use of polythene cloths raised into the air with the help of two poles can harvest about ten thousand litters of water from the fog called fog Harvesting either at day or night at the highest point as small pipes transport the droplets of water with the help of gravity down the slope for use. This was so impressive that I wish and plan for it to be introduced into my adopted locality of Madagascar. My first and foremost virtual voluntary work was rewarding that am planning to do that again somewhere around the world. Mr. Frost spoke at length such that Miss Hello was speechless and after he stopped; asked so, did it benefit the local people or the government of the country. The locals or native people and no one else... you should know by now that I dislike governments for, they can tell lies upon lies and inflate project budgets six times more than planned.

Can I also get too far on the meta? Oh yes, why not?...... on the Metaverse, look at the top right corner for the yellow icon which will display more than a thousand major places to pick from, and with each, there are another ten thousand places to pick from... it is limitless on the metaverse... it's as you like it or what you see is what you get Mr. Frost assured her. So, what about the Sulphur mines, what were you looking for, in the down below region?

The Youngins breathe in dry Sulphureous gas when they descend the mines about two hundred and twenty meters with the help of ropes and simple metallic tools. I joined a team of Youngins about sixteen to eighteen years old where at the rough edge surface of the mines which is about ten meters by five meters wide, we began to go down at a snail's speed with the air filled with Sulphur dust and heat from a wide and warm volcano vent. With a small breathing device purchased from Amazon online, I struggled to breathe freely as these Youngins managed to hold on to air in their young lungs for close to two minutes before another let go of air and even so, helped me go down till we got to the yellowish soil or yellowish rock which each picked as much as they can carry and began to make their way up in a full flight as if being chased by a deadly snake, well, I also did as I saw them doing with my small camera rolling events in real-time.

We surfaced within four and half minutes and at the surface began to call for air as some hurriedly dumped air into their empty lungs for life such behavior has a high toll on their health such that any can see it written on their faces. They had pale skin and malnutrition in hair growth, yellowish eyes, and wrinkles visible on their faces as if all were above the age of fifty-five years old. my knee did not hurt, my waist problem was a thing of the past as in the metaverse, each person or avatar is given an added advantage of what he or she can do and even do better. When the next team of miners entered the mines, they soon began to emerge out as they began to complain of an ancient demon below the mines which requires sacrifices each week to keep calm. To them, it's the god of the underworld but to me as a Westerner, it's a mild earthquake but they will not accept it. Alvaro Alvarez, a head miner in the company of two others reached out for alcohol to offer to the gods below and it was done by chopping off the head and neck of a black chicken whose blood was poured onto a small rock within the camp of the mines as they sing a certain song. An alcoholic sort of prayer was offered as with each drop of the alcohol poured on the bloody rock, they chanted some words to appease the ancient god below. I saw it as strange, very wild, and nothing so appealing about it despite not being religious in any way... Mr. Frost added.

As a journalist who has walked along the length and breadth of the diplomatic corridors of power, I intended to report all that goes on there perhaps, that will make the local and international power brokers of the world and industrial users of Sulphur boycott all Sulphur produced from Peru and to check the plight of the children. But also; in the twist of events, if the Sulphur would still be purchased from Peru, then it should be a proper mining activity with children being supported to start school again. I did my work and when I reached the World Education Watch, it was warmly received when the World Education Support project was very happy, the United States of American Committee on Education in Congress was happy but not the United Nations whose posture was we know about already, what else matters? I was hurt, I was mad yet ready to sting back at them with my work through other platforms across the world wide web. From that day, I understood that; some people can walk through a forest of trees and will see no tree at all.

So, whether this is an electronic dream or electronic magic, I can't say other to conclude that; it's a nice experience to behold and should I have come across this in the prime of my years as a journalist, I would have walked away from the slow and disappointing diplomatic arena of time, where it takes almost six weeks to make world events known to all concerned and about thirty-three days to attempt stopping a genocide and killings of local tribes in several countries.

So, with these experiences across the world, who are you when am not looking, baby boy? Hello asked happily... they looked straight into each other's eyes like old lovers trying to catch up and burst into a burst of wild and old laughter making Hannah peep at them as they sat all by themselves in the side corner of the visitor's hall. Margaret heard a screeching sound from a masculine voice and from nowhere showed up and only to conclude it was a guest visiting the Care Home for a reason.

In the not-so-far distant side of the world and the fine sand particles of the Sahara sits an oasis called Al-Yasin owned by the crown prince of Abu Dhabi Prince Moshed Al Rabin Nahyan with a personal net worth of eight thundered and sixty million United States dollars partly inherited and partly worked for in the oil-rich economy of the desert state. The oasis which lies out west of the capital has ten all-male servants, a seven-bedroom building built out of brown clay, and a nearby tent for the twelve well-trained security men trained in Britain and France. They made it to that part of the country on a fifteen-packed caravan of camel with provisions to last ninety-one days from water, food, seeds, date, sugars, bread, drinks and wines, rice and even guns and knives. Also; there was a streaming electronic device to detect approaching invaders ten miles away which was purchased two years ago for six million dollars from the French company during the Dubai arms expo.

Tee-minus five (T -5), they were schooled on what to feel within the first five minutes of lift-off from butterflies in their stomach, weightlessness and a burning sensation to warm and coldness. Again, all travelers saw each other, knew themselves and began to build bonds forgetting each other personal wealth, attitude as all that is wanted; is all that is needed as one for all and all for one. Health information and data for each person was sheard and other allergies as team work is more required than ever. Tee-minus four (T

-4), the flight pilots and engineers were named, show cased and introduced to their passengers as who does what was clear to all, on board is a flight commander, assistant commander, flight engineer, flight nurse, two flight astrologist, three Astro-electrical technician and field nutritionist. And the crew of eleven is all that is required to handle the number of travelers ready to launch out of earths surrounding for a season.

Tee-minus three (T -3), they walked in to the craft whose interior make up is as sleek and smooth as a British made Ross Royce phantom vehicle on the go. The Americans were the first followed by the Europeans, Africans then Arabians and Asian as each settled well in to his seat as per the numbers on ground. The all-men travelers almost looking like the Manchester City Football team in a bus to play an away match just that they were all outwardly silent but inwardly aiming to be there and to make a name for themselves. The flight commander, engineers and other crew members were to compartments away from them, checking, switching and testing the instrument for the very last time before lift-off into the known-unknown world of space.

Tee-minus two (T -2), seat belts were fixed and set, head set and inter-com sequenced and checked for every passenger as the commander began to speak to them and even cracking some jokes making al to smile and relax for what to come.

The assistant commander began by saying; an African class teacher in a class of fifty-five asked every student to assume all had survived a wild and sudden war that lasted for just ninety-one days with more a million people dead and gone either military man or civilian's person. Write an essay over what happened to you or how you survived. With that said, the talking and noise-making class went silent as each student began to write something making the teacher to breathe a sign of relief and began to go round and walk in between the classes only to discover a student writing nothing as his looked into the air.

The teacher then asked, my friend why not write huh?

Student: Sir, am not part, as during the war I was shot... so am dead. The teacher could not believe how odd and useless the student is by saying he was shot, so he is dead... he stopped the class and made all aware, a sudden burst of wild laughter filled the whole class lasting several minutes...

With that said, the team of travelers also burst in a frenzy as all became glad to be on that special flight...

Tee-minus one (T -1), the ground-based engineers, aeronautic engineers, space engineers, rocket scientists and air traffic controllers were all set to start the count to zero which marks take off. The door having been shut two hours back, the flight commander initiated the ignition sequence as his assistance began to turn switches on from right to left making several yellow lights to turn red and flashing for further attention.

- Engine light--- checked Engine sound--- checked
- Engine temperature--- checked Engine coolant--- checked
- Engine terminals---checked Leading edges--- checked
- Radio signals---- checked Inter-com----- checked

- Gyroscopic set-up--- checked Mapping plotter----checked
- Bearing readings---checked Inside temperature---checked
- Satellite communication---checked Compatibility ratio----checked

Start engines and apply heading at tee-zero for lift off, was the commander next order to his assistant which he accepted by saying yes Sir.

Tee-minus quarter (T -1/4), then the countdown began... ten, nine, eight, seven, six, five, four, three, two one... lift off. At a speed of ten miles per second, the rocket lifts its self-up and chasing the cloud above but in less than two minutes was out from view and moving away of the moving cloud which we all see and know about as the team was missing from human sight except with radio and other electronic communication devices reserved for the flight engineers to handle. The whole thing was on the news from British Broadcasting Cooperation (BBC), Cable News Network (CNN), Aljazeera, Russian Television (R-tv) and other leading news agencies across the world.

The craft lifted up, racing with its self far above the clouds at an astronomical speed of ten miles per second till with just twenty-six minutes crossed the stratosphere as all within the craft can now see the curvature of the earth and still moving and challenging the force of gravity. The first thirty minutes was gone, as the emptiness and dark matter was all over with outside heat increasing due to the sun radiations, in no time all were in space and all were happy and hopeful to see what others in the past million years have never seen or heard off. The common and silent moon was far away yet they were aiming ahead at it as by now the space craft was moving about eighty-eighty miles per second and they were in the middle of nowhere yet all were happy and cool as weightlessness is the very first thing that all experienced. Well, the moon which is about a little over a quarter of a million miles being three hundred thousand miles away was their target and the strategy is to move ahead of time in a semi-curve journey to meet it half way. The flight commander then broke his silence by saying; welcome to space and this is it, what is your take people? The warm beam of smile was seen in every traveler's face, glade and in fact their wealth has made it or have taken them that far as by now all can see the blue-pale dot which is diminishing in size for every second they move away from their position and towards the path of the moon. And it was true, the earth was in a suspending state, hanging and looking like a Walt Disney blue team balloon hanging on a high pole and with a side partly covered with white smoke which may be the huge clouds over the Congo or Amazon Forest. In a sudden bust, the engine stopped as its occupant's thing it might be a problem but instead the flight commander stopped for a reason, turned the craft about ninety degrees sideways and allowed everybody to see where they emerged from. They were floating just like the very world they emerged from which was also floating before their eyes even with the nuclear bombs, Heavy ships and submarines, high and tall buildings, even the pyramids of Egypt and the Himalayas mountains among others. The Africans on board, lovers of the cellphone and the internet were in heaven when their tablets were able to hook on to the interest in deep space as the smile on their faces were enough to alert all on what is happening on You-Tube.

From nowhere; a strange pack of sunflower oil fried plantain chips was passed around as each picked out a crispy fired plantain for his or her eating pleasure.

On the intercom, the commander's voice was heard alerting al to sit tight, buckle his or her seat belt... and when he was done and gone, the assistant commander or second-in command' voice was also heard where he said, "what the commander said was an order and not a suggestion" ... the engines was fired again as the space craft responded well now moving twice the speed of sound and almost catching up with the moon which from that point on, was like a white hanging watermelon heading towards their way. In less than five minutes the difference was clear as at this point the moon looks bigger than the earth, silent without clouds of its own, without trees and any living things which can move. At about seventy miles to the surface of the moon, although under the gravity of such a heavenly body, they applied their brakes and stopped. And what? The surface of the moon was very round and there wasn't a centimeter from where the stand which was smooth and clean. The hanging rock had its surface looking like the streets of Moscow, the capital of Russia just after the second world war. There was huge and open crates, hole and trenches from somewhere to nowhere and any would ask, so who did that huh? Hundreds of thousands of cone-like uplands which can easily pass as dead volcanoes, cylindrical and long dashing uplands almost drawing a line on the floor which can also be classified as mountain ranges which has no trees and even its steep valleys are so dry, much drier than the Sahara Desert on earth. One Arabian rich man asked, so; did Allah (God) create this one too?

One of the African looked to one of the flight crew and asked, so who own this now? Ahh, pleases what did you say? Was the response... I just want to know if the so-called Super powers of the earth, United Sate of America, Russia, China, Britain and even France; if they own land or real estate here too? And with that said, all in there began to laugh (ha ha-ha ha) at the African.

With that said, and they being in the world of their own, the highlands, mountains and uplands almost equal or higher than that of what we have on earth, then comes the trenches looking like lines produced by a child playing in the sea sand but then those lines are shallow long depressions which has uplands by its side and are said to be miles long from point to point. A trench stretching from New York to Utah or from Old York in Mohammed, the crown Prince personal assistant with a desert grade speed arrived at his location almost pushing him off his small red Turkish carpet and after just did not know how to make him aware or awake him from his electronic trance and not knowing what he is doing in there... the wind speed was up, the desert storm was high, huge and wild; also armed with billions of fine brown sand particles so fine and tiny such that, it can seal up the pores on the human skin and patched up the seeing eyes of both man and animals. After almost two minutes of long wait, Mohammed poked the crown Prince at his left side making him to move followed by pushing him a bit and it was that very push which drew him out of his space travel on the Metaverse allowing the rest to enjoy the Meta without him. His sudden surfacing on earth and what was happening was a bit scary as his allowed himself to be directed to safety and in that period and moment, the fast and huge sand storm was just on them and there was nothing any or even their technology can do other than to seek cover and protection from such ancient natural phenomenon which has wipe out a whole convoy or village before and none was arrested or queried for that.

And among them there was no wise man, magic power, royal decree, innocent saint, brave and strong man who has what it takes to shut down or stop what was happening... And truly, nature was ever stronger than science and the laws of man.

Even without timing, all or any can easily say the whole thing which looks scary lasted about two minutes long, two minutes of commotion and with that gone; there was a perfect five minutes of peace and total silence a kind of silence that can't be found in any part of the world not even the cemetery a place reserved for those we commonly say, must rest in peace.

Hamza, stood up after digging himself free from the almost one and half meter tall sand burial and began to dig out the camels which if they don't do that, these camels will die out on the desert within three days. Mohammed and the crown Prince were busy doing same, digging and freeing themselves from what has just happen as the crown Prince Oculus Head set VR can't be traced and even so, that does not look important for now. At the extreme side of the Oasis is a huge buildup of fine sand particles which a Sub-Saharan African may need to roast his freshly harvested peanuts for lunch. The huge build up sand particles will be about twenty-five trips load, a sort of mini sand dune but it fell short of burring the medium size water pond which feeds or refreshed all who dares to come closer even animals, from flying birds and insects on migration. The crew of men and caravan of animals were all dug out lasting about twenty minutes and a kind of phenomenon that was well anticipated as such none worried or complained as their vacation went on without any disturbance except that the crown Prince couldn't locate his Ocular headset to reach into deep space with the other billionaires.

The security team began to check for available water, and food that was around and in good condition, then worked on the animals which served as their vehicle and all were in good condition and finally began to set up and test their electronic devices to see if they have reception and can reach to base.

THE SAKURA

Norway; that white, cold, and silent country whose way of life is next to mind your business; filled with enough old people to warrant a Care Home; is an easy one lying on the other side of the world and that is that; but then what else matters? Tracy chanced upon it, as Margaret discovered it without knowing when they launched onto the Meta at a different period.

In the back end of the city of Oslo, is a place so dull, silent, and odd that even the Police Officers would not like to go there knowing all those there are but dumps and will do nothing to each other if even given a loaded gun to kill. Again, seventy-two percent of all gathered in there are women, sitting in that lone garden full of flowers once owned by the Lords of ancient Norway but now in the hands of these people silent, cool as if medically sick but none in there are sick and rejected by their fellow mortals. And if so, what is the problem?

The people in there arrived on foot some without gloves to warm their fingers only to sit around looking well into the open air as if there to await a deity from the heavens but that is not the case for, they are the loners, people who feels and wants to stay by themselves without any disturbance from any other. And conventionally, they have no children of their own. The almost six hundred and ten strong gathered people are the newest social group; an Anti-Social Social Club set by an unknown person called Milito. But why such a movement whose slogan is so odd and can make a healthy child get sick upon hearing it in less than twenty-four hours? Tracy was once there, Margaret knows them well as these two introduced Mary, Hello, and Hannah to the anti-social social club and truly a female-majority group. What are their objectives, their plan, what is their future goal and who are their executives leading the group? Will anybody say it, or who will be doing the talking? So, when all is set and done with some not in a good mood and others angry over something and would not want to speak to any, they dive deep into the metaverse just to locate the anti-social social club and with all gathered in their, there is no one either black or white, short or tall who speaks to someone in there and not even hello or hi…… And that is a fact people the very mood that they had in their minds is the same mood they exhibit in the Metaverse…… Oh, what a shame!

And on the open garden stands a white and blue flag with some words written in the Nordic language which when interpreted into the English language means "In my own Space."

Not that as they sit there; they are chanting, meditating, seeking something better out of loneliness but are just not willing to speak to anyone and very sure that; not even to their chosen gods of worship too. Getting into the garden also requires a fee of four Meta-cedi for regular visitors and seven meta-cedi for new attendees. In this multiverse of our common era, we have not just a Multiverse but a Universe, Metaverse, Macroverse, and Microverse which when explored well enough nobody will hear the cry and the calling of the other party at any given time.

This is life and what happens in life, is what life is. Well before she arrived at the front desk of the Care Home looking for a job, she just stepped out of an angry and wild relationship with an odd Police Officer who doubles as the father of her two children Andy and Lucy. In one case, he arrived well clothed in her uniform after spending thirteen minutes extra at her duty post and what was the point of spending an extra thirteen minutes to help a dying patient? She walked into the hall only to be rushed upon and slapped to the left cheeks by Stephen, her abusive husband but over what? With that done, he kicked her in the head, and in her attempt to get up and fight back, she fell only for the wild Policeman whose academy training was reserved to fight bad guys now being unleased on the mother of his children and beating her hard like an armed robber. The children chanced upon it, began to cry, and called on their father to stop but that did not work until Lucy picked up the phone and called 911 or the Police Department for help. The beating went on till the mother of the house went off, silent and perhaps in a trance as her body now submits to the abuse of Stephen, the so-called Police Officer, and her husband under the laws of the State. The long one hour which looked like a whole day to the children was odd, wild, and very emotional until a knock at the door was heard, as two Policemen whom he knows surfaced at his door and asked what is the problem not knowing who called them to his house.

And all was about the Meta-Dine Trade Expo at the Meta Strat City Center popularly called MSCC. Hippo-Star, the event organizer of the Meta-Dine Trade Expo is a virtual event organizer bringing people from all walks of life onto one platform for business and trade opportunities for top industry players from arms, construction equipment, manufacturing equipment, cloth and fabric machines, hospital and health devices, radar and aeronautic devices and many more. Despite its design for all to attend, nevertheless; it has been a sleek red carpet walk for millionaires and billionaires from the Arabians, Europeans, Americans, and Asians as our dear Africans mostly stay away as it is cash that does the talking. The African community of billionaires is small and the growing number of millionaires hardy patronizes such events except for sports expo, Conferences, and talk shows as development challenges still sting the continent.

The rich list from America and Arabia, the famous groups of Europe and Asia, and finally the political class of Europe and South America would be in attendance as the select few Asian royal passes through. The Meta-Dine Trade Expo at the Meta Strat City is situated in the North-East Hemisphere of District Seven which is an eleven thousand hectors state of the art Convention Center built for such activity with the ability to hold seventy-five thousand people with each dignitary given a space for his or her personal security detail to operate. The Convention Center has its stand-by power plant which is a backup to the main electric supply, water supply which also feeds the twenty-two fountains within the facility and the open area, and security department which allows a person each of every arriving or participating guest with a head high security team and a well set up Police Department for a level five security operation. Again; the Convention Center has a fire Brigade with three hundred and ten fire staff and seven fire tenders ready to work.

The maintenance and service department charged with electrical, plumbing, carpentry, masonry, and roofing system workers is on standby to do what they have signed for. The top organizers in their estimation had a mobile Polyclinic to handle first aid and emergency issues which may occur as seven doctors, fifty registered Nurses, and seven medical laboratory technicians in their cover cloths awaiting an issue. Despite the convention center being about fifty miles from the airport, there is a working airstrip that carries the sensitive and those with the ability to pay to be carried to the event grounds. Furthermore; there are many high-end hotels with some taking about twenty-five thousand meta-cedi per night; which comes with a personal butler, personal secretary, tour guide, personal cook, an Eastern European nanny, and added security team from which you would have the luxury to pick two men.

There were Seven registered hotels which were five-star hotels namely The Altrose, The Loom, The Cost Cutter, Mr. White, and Sam's Cottage with each with the ability to house three hundred and fifty high-paying guests with a six-car parking basement and a two-store house when needed to hold their staff and servants. Invariably, there were seventeen three-star hotels and twenty-two two-star hotels to fit the tight budget of others who require a place to lay their busy and tired thinking heads. Once in or after paying the fifty meta-cedi entry fee, other needs such as food, potable bottled water, and the use of the washroom are free at a point for which any who enters has been made aware, more so; the event managers have allocated spots to access special utility services such as electric rail transport which is also free and telephone calls within the Convention Center also free with the use of Internet and Wi-Fi.

And with all these, which movie actor or sports personality who is outgoing would not want to be there to see and to be seen? Well within the first day of lunch or opening, six European League football stars from Britain, Italy, Germany, and the Netherlands were there to shop, they signed a purchase agreement to send a particular piece of equipment to some selected Non-Governmental Organizations in Africa and Southeast Asia.

The agency mandated to oversee the sales of some selected blocks of items such as prime land, commercial papers, business authorization, oil rigs, oil blocks, pipeline paths accreditation, and others is Microverse. Microverse is a company backed with accreditation from the Meta-Quart the sole body serving as a framework to put in order the welfare of the Metaverse. With the authority, thereby making its own rules, and wealth and paying taxes as required, the Microverse leads the way well ahead of the others advertising or making all who dwell within and out of the Metaverse know what they do and what they have to offer. With a brief, they set the tone and the pace that, irrespective of who you are, where you come from and no matter the race or cast, either a Blackman, white man, yellow face or white face, Microverse is willing and ready to do business with you making sure what you pay for is what becomes yours without any governmental attacks from anywhere. With Microverse; "what you buy; is what you keep".

The South Americans from Columbia were the very first to set foot onto the metaverse followed by the Venezuelan nationals and the infectious Brazilians with millions to spend. They move in like drones as they walk across the red carpets in pairs as their security team stays close to their tracks and communicates with others behind the scenes. Alexandro Martinez with his wife led the way ahead of Ivan Marico another Columbian millionaire trading in stocks and commodities which same say, not all of his source of wealth can be traced to stocks and commodities like sugar, flour, Maize from Ukraine, sunflower oil from Russia and Sea Salt from Africa. Working with the Meta-Quart financial system they surfaced onto the Metaverse with six and a half million and ten million meta-cedi respectively and ready to buy and spend as they wish. Well after they were welcomed and taken to their respective hotels to settle down a new round of people also from South America was Lord Crostino a British-born Brazilian worth six and quarter billion United States dollars with her only daughter and two grandchildren all females, Petrov Alexis a Brazilian farmer with more than twenty-two thousand hectors of soy plantation at the south-east of Brazil arriving just two hundred meters from the Convention Center and on the ground of Sam's Cottage Hotel. They arrived in a grand style from the two separates; two hundred CC Embraer business jets with the capacity to carry twenty-five passengers then to a gold-plated Ross-Royce-driven car to the sleek grand hotel, in fact they arrived in grand style and they arrived rich irrespective of the financial pressure in their respective countries.

Then that, evening the European financial royals began to settle in also in their own Air Bus and Boeing planes making the airport fill up with planes, and trains of their self-owned expensive cars. In a step-wise direction, the Meta-Quart with its meta-power was up to the game from taking charges from all who dare surface with his or her train or fleet of transport from air traffic charges, landing fees, packing, and hanger fees for the airplanes, convoy fees and even currency conversion fees as they arrived with millions of United State Dollars. And when the Americans arrived, all knew they had arrived or they had the company of a sizeable size to contend with.

When Mary and Tracy surfaced to the Convention Center with their aims to see and know what was happening, they settled in with an economy ticket which was purchased about three hundred meters from the main gates of the event where financial royals arrive, only to be coached in a low-end taxi to their hotels which as at that time had no running water as there was a plumbing work going on in the basement of the hotel. They emerged from their hiding place the next morning and began to move around from stand to stand aiming at the health devices chances are they may recommend such a device to their employers and even so, are not the final determinants of the purchase order. They told their stories to the Brazilian company exhibiting their health devices which looked very attractive but had all instructions not in English. The Chinese stand was very standard yet a bit less on the pocket as with each purchase, one has the chance to free city tour at their expense. But the German stand was not so as they can only assure any of quality and quantity of production with after-sale service attracting thirty percent fee. At each stand, they pose like big players by presenting their case as it is and arguing and pointing some points out which even some have never noticed and their pointers were taken note of, they also left their company details or the details of the Care Home and other leading emails to the facility managers and owners living in London. Leaving contact cards and taking some also from them, all were happy with some ready to take them for lunch but they declined. They purchased items like fashionable pens, diaries, and face watches as towels, handkerchiefs, wallets, and ladies' purses were freely given to guests.

Just behind them was one of the Asian Crown Princes whose name is a jaw-breaking Malay name but then with a rich finger began to point and seek for what he wanted to buy as his travelling team was ready to help him with that. He asked for the military-grade drone whose price tag was nine thousand and two hundred meta-cedis, a one-mile personal protective radar which is mounted on top of your house sensing and making the operator detect every kind of threat about one mile away before it happens including the local weather readings. Then he paused knowing his personal account person would do the paying; for him to do the verification setups with the help of his cellphone. The screen presents other things that could not be carried down here was shown on the screen with military hardware such as air-to-surface launchers, surface-to-air rocket launchers to space, and other objects that even after paying would need military clearance before arriving in the respective country. By the German man was a small black suitcase whose content f not a laptop then what is it then?? When he asked, he was told it is a tactical chess reserved for military generals, military commanders, and even presidents of a country as with such a missile stock, one can target any country without physically going there. He made an attempt to buy that one too but was told such deals are conducted behind closed doors and should he need it, then they can organize it.

But then there was one part of the expo which is classically done behind closed doors and what is it knowing there is a tax component of the deal and it's a legal venture? The Microverse-XP, which is a subsidiary of the Microverse, and what is done in there is serious business. When the European Bank royal surfaced after stepping into the office, she asked for the selling price of the prime plot in slot-012B which is a three-hector prime land east of the City Center. Well, the lady coughed out six and a half million Meta-cedi, and that made the buyer smile. Well, what about four million meta-cedi upfront and paying the other in installments, what about that huh? That is a no-no for the company, we want full payment and that is it, she replied. Ahh, can I see your boss was the buyer's final words……

Furthermore, Jeff Stonewall a representative of Microverse-XP was processing the end of sale for another financial royal coming from mainland Europe to acquire the sale of the old gas pipeline which runs from Russia to Germany through Moldova at a selling price of sixty-two million Meta-cedi put on sale by the Stratazol Gas company which is Russian and Ukraine own and registered under the Federal lancing Law in Russia. After a rough negotiation by six people, they finally landed on fifty-eight million Meta-cedi for the three hundred-ten-mile-long pipelines with the ability to deliver sixty barrels of gas per second and with a life span of twenty years more after its sixteen years of usage. The sale of property includes lands, pipelines, and mega-hotel plots with beach fronts. other lucrative deals were up for grabs with the Americans and Europeans taking center stage well ahead of the others except for the Russian businessmen who were shopping passively until it came to the sale of the Islands in the West and East Indies and also in East Africa or the Indian Ocean.

Then comes Mr. Lukas Lucassen Popovich, a retired Russian Naval Officer who served in the first fleet of the Pacific who purchased a plot for a mega-hotel for forty-six million Meta-cedi two hours back readily placed it on sale just to buy prime land, an island of his own which in a long way will serve the Russian Federation soon. And well within the next three hours, an American bought it for fifty million Meta-cedi making a four million Meta-cedi profit in just five hours. Mr. Lukas Lucassen Popovich pressed forward and after losing six Islands al in the West Indies, he later got hold of one near Africa and not so far from the Island of Zanzibar, a two-hector plot which is actually a hill sticking out of the vast blue ocean and that will serve Mr. Popovich well as an old Navy.

Mr. Zhukov, the son of the late Air admirer of the Russian Air Force was there with a net worth of twelve and half billion dollars which can't be traced both in and outside Russia yet worthy of being called a billionaire and leads a lifestyle and acts as one. Without delay, when the small two-hector island was placed for sale at a price tag of one and half million Meta-cedi, all knew that that was too much and again a land so far from civilization which is about sixty miles from the Vast Island of Madagascar. Mr. Zhukov raised his left hand which has never worked like his late father and ancestors did, only to say I will take it. He paid the price, signed the documents that the United Nations and France have accepted to sell, and penned down his electronic signature that was it, Russian has registered his global presence at the tip of the deep blue ocean which France must observe and live side by side.

The Red-Star businessmen stray off from the prime city center lands, shipping lines that the Asian businessmen crave, the mega hotels that the Europeans love to own, and the oil rigs that the Americans toy with on the high seas. Despite the Red-Star businessmen love to work with oil, they picked the Floating Production Separation and Offloading (FPSO) vessel set-up for the oil rigs which is a sitting duck when it comes to global politics and events. Furthermore, one Russian explained, that the rigs; can't be relocated easily when natural disasters are about to happen on the high seas compared to the FPSO. But is that the real case or reason, one Italian Journalist asked back...

The only Russian who purchased something different was Maria Godowsky, a stock trader who purchased just one item from the MS Croft Shipping line with fifteen ships for seventy-seven million meta-cedi which plies the seaboard of South America and Europe; after just three hours of work or sale, a business transaction of six hundred and seventy-two million Meta-cedi has been conducted and still counting. The window shoppers coming from the Care Home were the on-lookers moving from point to point and buying nothing at all.

And there he sits, the Thai man from Thailand and the Red Neck man from the land of Russia sitting around the café table, looking at each other's cellphones as if attempting to help fix a problem but is that the case? Ludo Ing Mai the

Thai man is the deputy operation manager for Microverse-XP and Jeff Stonewall serves the company under his direction. For his second meeting with the Russians, what would they be discussing? What sale is about to go on and from what financial table have they been conducting their so-called business if not to evade tax or trying to trade illicit drugs... will a Russian buy drugs from a Thai? If not then; what is on sale and who is buying what? With their finger browsing touching the screen of the cellphone, seventy-six million Meta-cedi were transferred from one bank account to the other without using the SWIFT payment system but a dark-web paying plate form called Dark-Ages or (DAS) which has been in service for close to twelve years now and not even the European Union and the FBI has been able to break through after its discovery and again the Meta-Quarts is helpless in preventing its usage. And what was paid for huh? The men shook hands when the money reflected at the other end with text messages stating what or the amount which had arrived and from where it originated without the sender's name and other bank details which normally can help trace the person as smiles beam across their faces and with hopes that all is well.

When Tracy checked out of the Metaverse well ahead of Mary, she was welcomed strangely by the looks of Hannah, Margaret even John Iris Rawlings and Alex James Hyde making her ask what is it? Before Mary surfaced from the Metaverse, she was told that news was being circulated that, she was the girl lover of an American-Italian tax-evasive businessman having evaded tax for close to three years to the tune of ninety-two million dollars and the United States and the European Union is on a manhunt for him. Again, when two Policemen surfaced at the gate of the Care Home,

Hannah made them believe that they were at the wrong place and even added; will the girlfriend of a billionaire tax evasive man be at such a lonely place? And if so for what? The Policemen stood there and after using their electronic sweeper to detect and access every electronic gadget in the Care Home decided to leave and not to worry the old and retired senior citizens whiling their lives down till death comes for them. In total silence, Tracy was shut up, a bit silly, and did not know what to say in response knowing that it was not true, should she accept such an allegation and get attention and media coverage to make money out of that on YouTube or deny and be safe by hiding in her little cover as she keeps her job.

After a deep breath-in looked at all gathered there only to say, Oh yes... I took a picture with him at the trade Expo with two Policemen in the background... but that is all and who presented my picture to the tax authorities as it's only my cellphone that took the picture? Hmm, will it be that those Police Officers had somebody taking the picture too? Or somebody within the Meta hacked into my cellphone which was right within my care? Which is which and can that be done on the Metaverse too?

Well, I will think about it first but will certainly invest it into several financial instruments.

Well, hide and keep your activities low as any wild spending will make heads turn toward your direction at all times. But there, there they sit in total silence; am talking of those who can advise about when and how to hide, who to contact and who not to contact, and again what to use the money for due to their medical conditions like a duck on the surface of a ponding not knowing what those ladies who are not even half of their ages to keep talking and guessing what life should be; and John Iris Rawlings is one of them.

The nightly evening was cool but not free from problems as a silent family sedan pulled into the driveway only for two men to emerge followed by another middle-aged woman who after seeking the next step from the security man, stepped into reception with a yellow medical folder seeking to check-inn a new patient into the Care Home. Like a slow walking snail, the ninety-nine years old computer engineer and master of ethical hacking and Satellite communication who lectured at Harvard University and Massachusetts Institute of Technology (MIT) for twelve years and fifteen years respectively is crippled in his left arm and with only one eye with the ability to see is possibly weak such that he needs attention and can't be by himself for most of the time. The paramedical team who surfaced with him handed over to the facility head and the head of nursing or home care the yellow folder which has tones of medical instructions, feeding regulations, and varied instructions on what must be done for him to stay alive. Despite all these he is not a diabetic patient, a lactose intolerant person, and not entirely a neurological patient too but then what went wrong with him?

He settled in, looked around, and in a low faint tone asked where is this place? So, do you want to say that; you had no idea where they were taking you huh? Miss Hello answered...

The old man smiled upon seeing her face and went silent. Jack Volt had no biological child of his own and the two children he adopted are all serving as lectures in Osaka University and Hokkaido Technical University all in Japan as

System Engineer experts. The paramedic team finally served him with his old computer which is worth more than an electronic gadget in the Care home as he sat in his electric wheelchair only to turn the computer on and begin to seek wi-fi connectivity. He asked for the password which was given as Care_Home4U. like a crab at the seashore, he spent more than six minutes just switching on the computer and hooked on to the internet and after that; things began to go fast. He scans the whole area using some hacking soft wares which all in there have no knowledge of and then gets a bit of understanding of what lies within the whole medical facility and smiles to himself. From the IP address of their mobile phones, the health data system the other communicating systems, and security setups.

Mr. Jack Volt is physically weak but very strong, alert mentally able, and sharp. And come that evening, the ritual was on which is the taking of pills for their ills. Somewhere taking or swallowing the yellow and pink-colored pills, others were taking their shots or injections for diabetics and other neurological conditions. So, where are you from? Hello asked... Do you want to know where am coming from as to where I once stayed or which district is my personal information located in? Which is which Mr. Volt asked back? Humm, don't prove to be very intelligent that you are Hello challenged and looked straight into his face. I am Jack Volt and once a lecturer in computing before I arrived here, I was taken from Old York; does that satisfy you? Well, somewhat she accepted adding welcome to this place.

So, you are old or I can see that you are old; like any of us but does your mind tell you that you are old and praying that is if you believe in the Christian God and waiting patiently to die? I can see that am old but that is my human body and can respectfully say, that my mind has not even achieved a quarter of what it is capable of doing and as such is constantly working and able to do more than my human body can do... do you believe that? Yes, that is the point; the whole point... just that some here don't get it... Hello began to see that; she had come across a partner or at least one friend of the same mind and likeness. I am and still am a journalist very passionate about political issues that affect the world especially those in developing countries and adding my voice to what powerful people say behind closed doors in the corridors of the United Nations for which chances are they don't care about the crying masses in the wilderness of commerce and industry. Humm, you have been to places and you have seen events and occurrences which I can predict not all were you happy about isn't it huh?

Yeah, that is a fact my computer brother... eighty percent of decisions behind closed doors benefit the rich list of businessmen and women, the proud, the royals of the world, and the politicians but what about the low-class commoners of our world, they take from them their prime forest and lands, their minerals and power to vote all with tall promises which never happens and when they protest are gun down without the media allowed to telecast or broadcast what happened... what a wicked world where one percent owns ninety-five percent of all resources of the world. Why... I mean why should that happen huh? So, what can you do in our way if not to stop it, then perhaps change the narration of what is happening to your loved poor once across the world? Come on, think and do something Mr. Jack Volt said to her.

I can help with the computer manipulation and assign some friends elsewhere to help, can you provide the materials or the contents of how things should be? Volt added...

I also know there is something called the Metaverse which I have visited just once but know such a platform can be a game changer. May heads come together and may our minds which are the most powerful instruments of our time help.

The medical rituals were up again making the nurses administer the selected drugs as dictated by the physician to the patients in the care home which also begins the setting stage for the nurses to enter the Metaverse when their patients are put to bed. From the diabetic to the neurological patients with each taking not less than seven different kinds of pills for that night and every other night; like sacrificial lamps all were kind, quiet, silly, and had no chance to say a word making to be pushed off after just forty-five minutes after their medications and feeding.

And as Miss Margaret was in Russia, Miss Hannah was walking in the backyard of Ukraine two separate countries that were once one in principle and purpose but currently seem not so loved as their struggles are causing others in distant parts of the world to lament over bombings, deaths and killings, destructions, the hiking in prices of global commodities and it's the very poor who are feeling the effects. The farmlands which stretch as far as the human eye can see filled with corn, wheat, and sunflower are ready to harvest, several empty silos are just okay to store what would be harvested but then; the skies over these farms are infested with angry fast-moving airplanes with sharp knives and electronic arrows to kill, flying bombs intended to sail to elsewhere but with some landing in the vast corn and wheat fields making some farm harvesters to stay away. Farm animals that need watering and to be taken outside are now glued to their hiding places reducing in weight and value.

What is going on? She asked herself even with the fast-moving airplane scrapping the sky above but whose bullets and bombs were distant away from her present location. And, when one crazy bomb landed on the corn fields about ten miles away, a blazing fire was lit as with the help of the blowing winds, the huge farm began to self-destroy like the wild forest fires of American California, where inch by inch and yard by yard, the farm began to raise itself down in a speed set by the winds of Ukraine. She tele-transported herself to Odesa also in Ukraine with a population of nine hundred-ninety-three thousand and one hundred and twenty inhabitants whose oil industry is what helps to fatten eastern Europe from its sunflower plantations only to be greeted by uniform men and not even one was a woman perhaps, whom she can easily called upon, they held in their strong hands guns which can kill and even kill the human soul, they have cutting knives which is fashioned to cut open with the least of human effort and they had ugly cars whose strength as a machine is more than seven thousand horses put to work on a corn field but what is happening?

She asked herself, is this a city, a town, or a war zone, and if war zone what is the fighting for? And what is the set-aside prize to the winner of the war and to be given by whom? Odesa was a bit cold, with several others wishing to leave but to leave to where. And if others are leaving what about her who is not a native of such a city? She found herself in Kyiv, the Capital and political powerhouse of the country, and thinking she would receive a warm hand as the cold winter was fast approaching, she was met by a city which was fast asleep of a sort, streets were empty, street lights were turned off, buyers and sellers where on a kind of vacation as the visible water fountain had no water to slash around. Even the small little birds that normally fly across the city square were nowhere to be found, a mystery which needs to be solved as uniformed men with armed military hardware were all over protecting and defending the city but from what and from which direction? Is it Russia, the world's oldest foe or ally? The guns were pointing not down or up but sideways with their index finger ready to press or squeeze the trigger to he who claims is worthy to take what is rightfully theirs.

The city was partially dead if not in a medically induced coma, silent, sick, and needing attention for every passing hour as men who should have stayed to do just that; were leaving allowing the selected few to do just that. She then asked where are the men? Where are those who do or perform the art of decision-making without involving the women and when things go wrong will be wheeling the women along as if the women are part of the problem, where are they now? And the city of Kyiv was begging for help, was begging for support but not on her knees.

TABLE OF MEN

The Meta-sphere or the Metaverse was designed to present another session of life experience where each person will be given a chance to be of good behavior and to serve his or her community as this life is not meant to be enjoyed but to serve and to be purposefully useful to your community or society and country.

But is that the case or has it been explained to all who dare venture onto the Metaverse or not? Each has been given a degree of living space upon which should you do well, extra space would be given such that; there is Meta-Das from which Meta-Dash is next. Meta-Quark is the highest and the most prestigious location to dwell, see it as a sort of seven-star hotel where apart from the initial payment to be hosted, nothing is charged again for a whole week or one hundred appearances onto that platform, and those in there are of a royal status to behold and no wonder their names or the list of them is not readily published for all to see.

There are no Youngins or old folks here as any who dare settle down here are worthy and accepted to be but does that mean in a seven-star hotel, all who live in there unacceptably made their money, or are all Saints and righteous as such? From one level to another level is by merits but with the help of others behind the scenes, which can be classified as having Meta-Craft has been able to admit some high-paying individuals like Crown Prince and financial royals across Europe, Asia, and the Gulf regions who are known to have bad manners through the back door without the authorities knowing what is happening and if even they know, once they have successfully checked inn; it is very difficult or impossible to push them out.

When John Volt checked into the Meta at the same time with Hello, they were in the prime of their youth only to be greeted by another youngin in the basement of a bar doing his own thing with his laptop. Ahh, stealing on the web, isn't it? Hello said. I stand with Ukraine he said and as a computer student will do all that lies within my power to shake Russia with my online friends... But by doing what? John asked... by hacking into their systems, plant viruses, and electronic warms to either slow down or scatter their information about and that is what we are up to. We, who are we here? Can you explain boy...

At the United Nations and other bodies of Nations, be it Commonwealth, African Union, North Atlantic Treaty Organization (NATO), European Union, Arab League, and the rest; there is always a table in fact, a working table on which all sits around but only important issues and significant signatures gets sign on; as such making others to call it the moment of truth; do you believe that? Hello began to lecture Jack.

The working table, around the working table, are people in black well well-pressed coats who call themselves career diplomats working for the welfare of the nations but then, doing several side jobs and consultations with other nations and organizations with whom their nations have paid them not to work. Well before they left Kyiv, they came across John Cool another seasoned journalist who has a bit of diplomatic keys and has seen and worked with other institutions for close to twenty-five years and is ready; not afraid to say what lies within his mind. He called on Hello who was quick to open up to him and also introduced Mr. Jack Volts making a smooth friendship to pick up, and when he heard of the topic being tables, he smiled and began to talk too.

What happened just after the Second World War as written by historians is the very same thing that happened in Rwanda, the South Sudanese region, Yemen, and even Syria, and it will happen again. And what is that, what is it that will happen again? John Cool kept saying... at that table which is the working table is an inner table being "The of Men and the Table of the Ordinary". And what is the difference here? Jack questioned. The Table of Men (TOM) comprises the big guys, the big players, and those who are at the top of the food chain where every move that they make affects their national companies or companies registered in the good books of the country's company registry and whose tax goes to that particular country. Should they make a point, it's in favor of those companies whom their citizens own. Such countries are America, Britain, France, Russia,

China, and other European big players in the corridors of power.

Besides that, the next set is the table of the Ordinary and they are those members of the United Nations who do not matter and never will matter in the distant future when it comes to voting in the Security Council and making decisions to stop and start a war. They have little to no financial power freedom and resources to go a separate way, again they lack the political will to make policies that will positively affect their nationals and are always at the mercy of the top five countries in aid to support their yearly national budgets. With some, chances are; they live under the table or are under the very influence of the table of men (TOM) and their policies are never a policy but either to say "Yes or No" to what they are told behind closed doors within the cabinets of the United Nation offices. Just think about it, please don't ask me to list such countries for they are all over Africa, South America, and some East Asian countries. The whole thing looks like some were created to live as others were created to exist by the same Creator. To Africans, so sorry to say that; they are nobody within their own country and nobody outside their native countries too, they are equally nobody before TOM.

Table Rules (TOM)

To African and other third-world country diplomats and political Leaders across the corridors of power at high places.

1. Do what we say and not what you think.
2. Once under the influence of TOM, fear nothing.

3. Gently sign the trade policies and we will do the rest.
4. Get in touch and we will bear the touch.
5. Soften your home media and feed them with yours.
6. Hold on to power only at our request.
7. Keep them constantly poor, it's our goal.

With this well-enumerated sentence construction, Jack looked at John as if he just surfaced from Mars, an alien which must be made known to the North Atlantic Space Authority (NASA) or the United Nations (UN). Ah, is that true, and what was your reaction and what did you do as in protest for all these years? Jack said. Who am I, and what can I do when the big fishes of the deep sea are fighting and arguing for what they want? It's like standing in front of Joseph Stalin of Russia and asking for a pardon for Adolf Hitler of Germany. Had it not that I went quiet and down below the table, I would have lost my position and the key which makes me cross the carpet to cover some of these high-profile events and meetings within the United Nations. But this is what I have gathered all this while. John added...

You see from afar when these politicians surface on our televisions, they appear to be all-knowing and with the swing of their pen can fix every problem that lies on the surface of the earth but not knowing they are the very people fermenting the problems only to be swept out from office leaving the problem for another politician who will add up his faults and ill ways to the already difficult problem which his fellow mortal faces every day.

Well, before he could say a word, the transfer was over, and within a fraction of a second John Cool stopped him in his tracks adding... should you be quick in pointing out these things, you will end up being stabbed to death. By the way; are you the Police and if even you are, is stopping these people the very job you have been paid to do? Come on, wake up man!!

These Youngins, whom I don't want to say, come from North Korea but look more like the people who come from the very country where North Koreans come from... I think that is the point. These Youngins were as busy as a foundryman in the best of times doing his work with hot metals.

Once the deal or transfer is done, the whole room lights up with white flashes that last for just sixty seconds, and with that, no one in the room can say did not see or feel what just happened. Then from the far side of the second lineup of computers numbering about seven was a lanky Youngins whose hairstyle looked more like haven't seen the blade for close to ten years on a role and with enough human hair to pass him up as wildling of the West. Calm and steady, not looking anywhere, and with fingers punching and clinking as fast as possible was what made him stand out compared to the rest. His fingers kept typing, coughing numbers, and picking instructions as fast as they popped up onto the screen, and with that, all was done and all was set as he was working not only for his daily bread but for his survival with such a group ordered and under the inspection of the Interior Minister who reports directly to the Dear Leader and Ruler of the country. He has no dollar to his name yet except afternoon and evening meals and a bit of favor according to his family for working for the Dear Leader.

Jack Volts was shocked and a bit disturbed to see a sort of state-sponsored hacking program with the state security set up or asked to give them protection. Hacking tools like Dark-Core-Ages, Knox-Ville Web, Skull Master, and Bone-Boom-Tee whose country of invention or origin is not yet known. But, can this also be used against Nasa or the Pentagon? What about the British Scottish Yard security setup?

A mean minimal or marginal amount is always taken from companies with active financial accounts and whose daily transaction is so huge that any marginal amount will never raise a question mark and no tired neck of an account will turn to see what just happened.

The Koreans faced Youngins in the basement and called themselves Pai-Tee Group working in shifts and there wasn't a time that there was no person behind the computer and make sure no matter the time zone around the world, they were in a position to work hard. Like an African blood-sucking mosquito, the small number of Youngins working hard and well like a well-oiled moving part of a machine can pick up and transfer about twelve million dollars per day and that has been their work from the very day the group was instituted. When Jack looked into the calm face John, thinking he would say something but all that he did was; smile making Jack ask if that was not a bad and criminally minded act huh? Well, State-sponsored hacking and State sponsored terrorist acts which is good, and which is bad? Or better still which one gets innocent people killed and which does not?... please talk... John added.

But, but... why?? Jack lamented again as Hello looks on...

The world is not fair... Jack said, only for John to answer that; the world is equally not dark in complexion too...

On this Metaverse, there is Meta-quart, Meta-terra, Meta-zone, and even Metapol and with all these what is their work huh? Can't they arrest these criminals or is this State different from other States? Jack went on talking to his friends. Well, for those regulators...yes, they exist... and you must blame every leaking way or weak process on the Table of Men (TOM)... they caused it and within the high levels in the United Nations there is a silent saying that "To every front door, there is another back door."

The state-sponsoring hacking is real and already happening, as the United States of America; and the World Police sit unconcerned. Something must be done fast. Come, dude, you better question your belief system as the World Police which you know is the very person leading the charge on the Table of Men (TOM).

At one end of the Meta, all seems well, and possibly there is a clean sheet for all to write on except a small section of people which are of two kinds, the TOM and the Youngins daring the system and trusting no one no matter what happens. Apart from the Dark-Core-Ages, Jack saw the Skull Master put to work; this is a hacking software with the ability to detect, wipe out and even copy every possible information on military computers and systems, and currently, those that they were working on that of African countries and I mean all of them knowing the range of weapons, capabilities, man strength, ongoing projects and their available cash to spend and with this information gathered, its then sold to Asian and Western powers at a fee. The set of Youngins who are not in uniforms or belonging to a set-up military wing, have clear-cut military information which is at par with the American Pentagon and the British military intelligence on Africa and some selected South American countries including Brazil. From a point with not a dollar to their names, now each person in this group has something to die for and that is a fact, people.

Jack Volts was disturbed, speechless, and wished he could do something and if not to stop them, get the information over his country from their very hands and can that be huh? After a deep breath-in said, what can I do to help you boys? Making all t turn their heads a bit... well if you want to help, how will that be? We know you Sir; one began to speak out... you are a computer grand master and worker of codes and linking; is that not the case? Yes, you are right, what can I do? Jack seeks patiently as Hello and John looks on.

And at what fee? And what will be your charge per hour Sir?

May my fee be that any nation can be touched but my country would be spared... was his request for which Miss Hello jumped into the conversation by saying no, what is so special about your country? Is that country of yours not part of the permanent security group of countries within the United Nations? Is he not as sinful as others and if so, what is the point here, man... Do you better ask for something better or nothing?

The curious Hannah and evading Mary stepped into a new corridor in a certain county where the rules for men are as equal as the rules for women making any in that country question who is God and what he stands for. In that setup, one can see women engineers, men registered nurses, women serving as political leaders and men being midwives at the health care centers. And none in there was hurt, alarmed, and worried over nothing except the threat of invasion from a worthy fellow whose arsenals have been pointing toward them for close to fifteen years now. To them, every person is a fighting tool and every person is the able equipment to fight off the invader should that happen making several people have more than two skilled jobs all in favor of their dear country and their faces too look like Koreans but so sorry they are not Koreans. The name of the game was the Meta and the rules of that very game is the Meta as the stage is the Metaverse on which several acts are produced even TOM... as points on the stage are the Micro-verse, Macroverse, and the rest.

Miss Hello checked into the top files of the New York district without knowing what she wanted but after just ten minutes stumbled upon the criminal records of the Banker Anthony James Keelson formerly of the Finch Bank. He robbed the bank of about fifteen million dollars over five years which took close to six years to identify and after his conviction and sentence was taken to Grayson County Prison where he will be spending close to seven dry months in confinement. Well, that is not entirely the news here; a grey wine and former Police superintendent now on retirement was quick to point out that this very case was the most useless case to ever be televised for the entire country. And what is the point?

Listen up Mom; high-profile individuals, their friends, cronies, family members, and other business associates are quick to pay the jailer such that; the general public may think he is behind bars but instead is secretly hidden in a mansion out of town with the best of amenities and even given some wayward women for conjugate services for a fee. These high-profile criminals are a little economy to the jailers where money is dole to them per week to keep such people free from the shackles of the prisons for as long as possible. Do you believe that huh? The retired Police Superintendent went on, he took or fished out close to fifteen million dollars from clients' accounts, and it is in bits such as ten one dollars, five twenty dollars, twenty-two dollars, and all these amounts when multiplied by the number of people, that is huge per month, just imagine taking two dollars from two hundred and fifty thousand customers bank account which is so small an amount that; they will never come asking for it... and this multiplied by two hundred and fifty thousand dollars is about five hundred thousand dollars of free money and that is the work of an account who also has the best of computing or hacking skills.

Drinking, smoking, sleeping rough with their co-girls, and doing what best fits the day with money coming from their contract givers in high places within several organizations and even TOM is not innocent from this very group. He arrived at the second level of the station reserved for abnormal times such as war and other natural disasters with handshakes, all settled in knowing their rightful place with the group; after that, there was total silence for a minute only for a handsome man perhaps coming from the Applied Physics faculty in the University of York only to stop and began to spill out his words like a radio presenter at the British Broadcasting Corporation (BBC) radio. His second sentence construction was as follows; "the Cut-off offer for the Two-Star-General commanding and leading the second Infantry battalion has been increased to ten million Meta-cedi". May the "Excominicato Operation" be hastened as per determined.

He busted a drug syndicate that circulates drugs to children between twelve years to thirty-two years old and whose street value is worth eight-seven billion Meta-cedi. His life was secretly hurting as now his cover had been blowing off, his wife and children were not able to walk chest out in public and his name was on the lips of all calling him a new fund hero but such a label was hurting and killing his real nature. The ring leaders were detected, picked up, and arrested by the Metapol; as the politicians were named and shamed.

The Strategy officer serving within TOM who also doubles as the Prime minister of Japan had a company operation in the deep waters of the Philippians and the United States of America, but is that all? Posing as a fisherman and hired to work for MV Jotter, a deep-sea fishing vessel sailed deep into the blue waters fishing, picking, and hunting fishes from the open ocean only to come so close to another fishing vessel named MV Blue Canal packed with strange wooden containers with holes to allow air in. MV Jotter blew her loud whistle to salute her for which she also answered but after five hundred seconds as we were fishing, another big fish showed up and drew closer with her boom began to pick off the strange wooden containers but then which animals were in those boxes, which animals are they trafficking? And is that right? The Metapol officer laid low and did his work until the authorities aware of who stopped the illegal work not in wild animal trafficking but human trafficking where they served elsewhere as sex and domestic workers. From stopping the sale of fellow humans which brought the end of the Prime minister of Japan to gambling and other dirty works along the perimeter of the Metaverse.

But the worst was the Giscard Avenue at section fourteen-side A of the Metaverse. There was a wide range of Youngins between eleven years old to about twenty-two years old smoking, sipping, sapping, and drinking their lives away think it's a new form of lifestyle and manliness including the girls with some whose parents are political figures in high positions. Gambling was another but with gambling, it's just money which can also be called paper after all, it is stolen or dirty money but when it comes to the art of drinking adulterated alcohol which will weaken, kill, and break down their internal organs it is very worrying and deadly. With an industrial chemical used in tanning work and popularly called Grey-White; a high percentage of large drugs, dropped into the huge volumes of alcohol and left to settle for six hours only to be refilled and sold in a volume of seven hundred and fifty miles; commercially called Strong-Mann or Siberia-Grey.

They drink their strength away as with some especially the ladies emptying six bottles of this kind of drink per night starting from ten o'clock afternoon and three o'clock into the early morning; only for their drivers to take them home as ordered by their parents. Despite being a Metapol and not scientific; he gladly concluded that they kill half part of their inner soul per night. And with this, he did not report it, and no one heard it as their parent did not just know, but they are part and parcel of their children's personalities as they are constantly not at home to correct them leaving that part of the child to bring to the house helps and other servants paid to do a different job in the house.

And with all these, was he promoted? No... Salary increased? No at all... Given medals? No... Given any benefits? Hell no... so, what was the point of going that far to risk his life and making his reputation to be on the negative side of life? Well, his name was Jon Chalk.

Then just like every civil servant, there comes a time when his time is due to go home, to take the stage to things that matter for another young soul to replace the role; well, not to rubbish the whole process, it has been given a fair name called retirement. He was sent home and pushed out from the payroll of the Metapol. Jon Chalk was sent home without a recognition or citation...

The Table of Men (TOM) was at its position, doing what best suited them as the large masses kept walloping in poverty with the intake and abuse of drugs ever increasing, and who cares... There was a door, there were rules and regulations well outlined by the Meta-Quarts with several institutions to enforce and uphold them in high esteem as TOM glides behind the scenes working the arts of silliness within their black sleek suites... the table of the Ordinary starts from the millions of Youngins drinking and smoking their lives away, civil servants dividing and breaking rules to suit their interpretations and how to benefit from it as the small section of people being the physically challenge hoping against hope each time. With his children gone out of the house, and whose educational fee he must bear for the next six years; he quickly pulled out his pen and white paper only to draw up a plan, a plan to get back to work again. And that was how he produced his application letter to Comza-5 Private Security Company. Jon Chalk is the type who easily goes by the saying "All Shall Pass."

When he met John Cool that faithful morning after submitting his application letter, it was an instant jackpot of friendship as Mr. Cool easily noticed who he was and what he did for the Metaverse. So, Sir; how is life after retirement? Well, just submitted my application letter to seek a new job not that I wanted but my meager salary of six hundred and seventy Meta-cedi can't walk me and my family through the month without borrowing to top up... he said without shyness.

The noise level began to compete against the outside world which is from the birds and by so doing, Hannah was quick to tell them to try their best to reduce it without stopping their work too. As for the Carpenter, the up-and-down reminder from Hannah was never taken as the procedures of his work were more important than what the nurse was saying. Then the painters went away followed by the plumber the very next day with the rooms partly in order as the final person the carpenter must add his side of the operation.

With that out of the way, the Head of Facility management arrived to check what had been done making all other nurses to be responsible that day and even hiding the Ocular Quest Vr device as Mr. Jack Log went up to do that and well within fifteen minutes all was over, assembling the nurses, he asked so what do you do at your spare time huh? Not so much Mary began but was quick to add, that we would be glad to have the newly introduced device called Ocular Quest VR for us to not just see the place but visit such a location. Well, I will table that to management and hope they buy into that; which if they do, I would personally buy one for you people... with that said, all cheered and were happy as the patients looked on with indifferent moods except Miss Hello White whom Margaret was praying in her heart that she should keep her mouth shut and never to say anything. As for Jack Volts, well never mind... the plumbing work was good as the out-ward vents and pipes now look good with waste-water running out freely, likewise, the carpentry work made the whole room look like it was just out of the world of antiques. The painting and polishing up was good, using a kind of technology paint which once the walls are dirty normal water and cloth can be used to wipe or clean it up.

And when the Anglican seminary team surfaced, just like they said in their letter dated September in the year of our dear Lord; they surely surfaced in a parish sedan car with two Toyota caravan cars filled with a content best known to them with smiles and hopefulness to see the workers and occupants of the Asda Care Home, a privately owned and controlled care home belonging to retired health worker called Genesis Cynthia Bedrock. Led by Bishop Japhet Patterson, the Parish Bishop of Lille Wood a community of one thousand and twenty-two strong faithful to the church surfaced with glad tidings and freebies for the Care home as one of their being Mr. Jack Volts was there. They presented themselves to the facility care manager who invited other nurses and even assembled some patients but was quick to add that; the institution does not permit taking pictures with the patients except those of their own family. They spoke or said hello to all who said nothing in response except Miss Hello and their man Mr. Jack Volts.

The visitation of the Conference for Ministry of Magic is held once every four years in the city of London; where all participants irrespective of age, gender, aura, and charm present themselves before the Grand Master of things which are meant to be; to showcase a learning of a new skills or an add-upon marks of difference in the society of theirs; so was the addition of Oculus Vr meant to them at the Care Home. With the security man doing his part, the Nurses with their patients can take a walk into the Metaverse to showcase to each other the stuff that or she is made of or what he or she can do. Hannah, Mary, Margaret, Tracy, and other cooking staff and laundry staff can be part of the assembly. Two nurses, trained in dietary namely Jane Jones, Sarah Stopper, and Stephanie Johnson all of whom came from Lister School of Health Care also in York were welcomed and not new to the use of Oculus Vr. Nurse Hannah reached for the device only to display what was written around it which reads, produced by in China Hanan Province for Samsung Electronics Company Limited, South Korea. With the sudden joy like; the blast of the Volcano on the big Hawaiian island, they yearned to start the use of it despite knowing powering it up for close to three hours to prime its usage.

She looked keenly into the seeing eyes of her patient Alex James Hyde and went like... I am prepared to take care of you, don't Screw up on me. She did as tell, cleaned him up, clothed him, and wheeled him to the table for his medications which were six different pills from pain killers, antidepressants, immune system busters, cholesterol reducers, cough syrup, anti-inflammatory drugs all from the Consulting physician. And well within two and fifteen hours, they were all brought to stay around the table to eat, swallow their pills then allowed to watch the television. When the landline rang, the nurses thought it was for any of them but after picking up the call it was the grand-son of Rawlings wanting to speak to his grandfather whom he had seen physically once and wished to talk to him this time on. And when the call was transferred, Jayson Banks called to his full name as if he is his co-equal... John Iris Rawlings; how are you? I am calling to check on you Grand-Papa...Are you okay? Jayson added knowing his grandpapa has a bit of a hearing problem and, as such kept on talking knowing he couldn't answer back. Please I will show up to visit you soon and be a good boy Grand-papa... bye then; the line went and with the nurses taking the receiver from him, he began to smile as one nurse asked; so, what did he hear at all?

In the news, it said that; three armed robbers with American-manufactured machine guns each rushed into a banking hall with the sole aim to get some money and run off in a short period. And with that done in their first thirty seconds, little did they know there were two military off-duty men in their civilian clothes whom the very last time they saw action was in Iraq... and in as much as the action picked up, they presented themselves in a military ambush maneuver. Just as the first gun spits out its bullets, the first man whose name is not mentioned reached into his top pocket only to pull out a writing pen, went down as if about to obey them but within a swift second; drove the pointed part of the pen well into the left eye of the first robber throwing him off balance and taking his gun from him only to shot him in the head at close range, well... his bloody body fell like a cut-off log in the nearby forest. The second military-trained man like the first drove a pencil which he was about to use to write for his small boy before they entered into the left side of the second robber's neck making precious blood gush out in an air spray all over the place and with that done punched him hard to his nose and that was it as the man with the gun went down and sitting flat on the floor with the gun in his right hand not able to shoot at anything after his open declaration... "Fuck off and lie on the floor with face down"...

The third person who left the black Benz car with its engine on was greeted with two shots to his chest and that was all for the day. The whole thing happened well within two fast-flash minutes of panic sounds and crying. Nevertheless, the banking hall was still and silent starting from those dead robbers except, for a mentally confused and disabled man on the floor whose blood kept pumping out of his body through the neck with every breath and once on the floor the blood steams away like a silent red river from its source to the low plains and even any untrained eye can conclude that he is dying slowly.

The room then became cold for close to five minutes but only to those who could hear and those who heard the exchange as the rest kept looking at the moving pictures on the big screen by the wall. Miss Stopper without a sign to comply with began to wheel the old folks one after the order to their rooms and help them get to bed. First was Hyde followed by Rawlings and then Wood where for each she spends seven minutes to transfer them to their beds with the help of Miss Johnson from Kenya in Africa. Windows closed, curtains sealing every view from inside, bedside television turned off, lights off doors well secured, the nurses left the room knowing all was well with the patients for the next twelve hours. But then the partial stroke patient who has injured himself twice in the bathhouse in the attempt to use the washroom is keenly monitored with circuit television to assist him in urinating as he normally does not put on pads at night. For all. The night was upon them and all had a choice either to shut their eyes or do the otherwise.

In the perfect nature of the Metaverse, when all things are made right with orders underlying every detail which was and which is to come; the days of all were predetermined and preorganized as such. The Sixteen Oracle Square was packed and well-filled with all those who matter and hold not just power but grace which is accorded every living person on the Metaverse. The Care Home nurses were easily dazzled and drawn to the colors, shapes, and beams of light; of the moments as the events kept calling people from far and near within the earth sphere to show up. The Africans, Asians, Americans, Europeans, and even the Ice landers were there too. And when Jane Jones, stepped onto the red carpet below the long flight of stairs; ...... there she saw, Miss Hello White in her true stature, colors, and intelligence as she was in the company of media moguls from Australia and India discussing what best suits them. Well, perhaps it's this which makes her look down upon all... what an old lady to be with... Miss Jones commented. In less than two minutes other nurses from elsewhere show up only to sit next to her table. From nowhere Hannah and Stephanie Johnson showed up only to sit with Jones at the same table wot far from the event center point.

Alex James, the Civil Servant was there but in the best of forms, from masculinity, heritage hair, muscular body, and the ability to fix broken items easily. His dementia and nervous problems were gone, and even vanished into thin air; with newfound abilities and capabilities, he looked around and went like... yeah, yeah... God is great. Making all know his Baptist heritage. With the ability of almost settling in, a strange but familiar man began to walk towards him at the best pace of steps with bare hands and a calm face. Thinking of a knife stabbing about to take place, he began to take some steps back only for the man approaching him to wave his hands and add his name as am; James Lower, am one of those you trained Sir... can't you remember huh?

The nature of the Metaverse was such that, all within the platform of the Meta irrespective of height, race, religion, social and political affiliation of any country on earth, rich or poor, royal or a commoner, scientist or a school dropout; and no matter who you are, as far as you show up onto the Metaverse, you are but a new creature able to do wonderful things for yourself and by yourself. Alex James or AJ, the retired Civil Servant as he was well known; began to see from point to point old and great friends whom he had lost contact with since time immemorial and truly he was happy to be seen and to be seen.

They talked, about a few things and many other things which as a bedridden person, he could not say, and after all began to shed tears for a new experience and ability to see all including the hard-core Tony Wood and asking where that lady called Hello?

As soon as her name was mentioned, she appeared; Miss Hello White the all-knowing and kind of pupil-teacher to the Nurses trying her best to school them in all that she knows surfaced to the surprise of all as she now saw them in their true elements. And what are you people looking at huh? She began to question thinking she was old but not knowing Mr. John Irish Rawlings was five years older than her age but was always full of gratitude to the hard-working nurses who could pass as his grandchildren back home. Am not your standard fellow so, be careful... by the way what brings us here people? She asked wanting somebody to reply to her...

At that point, Mary now understood why the Metapol asked him of Tony when she surfaced. The sound of the siren called other Metapol cars to get involved with the chase and there was none with pity towards the driver in the front seat of the black sedan car. But did any know he was a robber and for that matter a bank robber? The black sedan was heading towards District Nine a populated area where there have been more than two thousand Youngins located part-ing, eating, dancing, and doing all sorts of things typical of most youths on earth and with a speed of one hundred and sixty kilometers per hour, the Metapol was worried and no wonder the Metapol helicopter was above was trying to snipe him out of the car. The first shot from above was shot but hit the front passenger side of the fast-moving car as the chase was on and wild. He crossed the Yolo Interchange in just eleven seconds almost like a ghost as all the cars who saw his passage were very worried about why the Metapol should sit down and watch. He jammed into a green Toyota family car hurting a mother and baby on board and without stopping zoomed off leaving the motionless mother and a crying baby in the car.

The fifth shot hit the back car tire which did slow the car but did not stop and after sixteen seconds the other back tire was deflated for the next two minutes the car stopped under a bridge and that was all when the Metapol arrived, he was nowhere to be found making them launch a full-scale manhunt for the robber, killer and traffic offender at another level. The Metapol detective Peter Sam Wong, rallied his men and in his short address said the robber too to the woods adding he wanted search or sniffing dogs, all man hunters, animal hunters, patrol guards, and an air patrol search team to get him man and he needs him within twenty-four hours. Well, dismiss and get busy was his last word.

Man, men, and animals were at their best doing what they have been trained to do for years now as in no time sixty dogs began the search with their keepers and other Metapol guards with weapons to hurt and to kill.

With all under way, Margaret from nowhere surfaced and not knowing what was going on, complained to the rest that; the place was too noisy and what was the matter. Well, Tony Wood is on the wrong side of the Metaverse as the Metapol officers were after him if not his head. Jones added. After just two hours according to the Metaverse local time, a trail was detected making all others begin to converge at a point but when the Chief Detective of that district heard it, he was a bit angry adding that what if it happens to be a wrong trail? Stanley Murry then charged that no stone should be left unturned and that made other locations to be looked into again allowing a small armed number to zoom in into that area. The dogs began to bark but it was the very barking or sound of the dogs that made the suspect aware that he had company one Metapol said to the others about two hundred meters away from the location.

Well before they moved, the Metapol cars began to approach only for them to see the arrest of the ring leader of a bank robbery which had four of the robbers killed and two Metapol officers killed. In an attempt to get away from three million meta-cedi, they were engaged by the killed Metapol officers who made other officers aware, and after a thirty-two-minute gunfight; he is now under arrest after six hours of manhunt. And that was Tony Wood a seasoned robber and a person having escaped twelve robbery operations. He was arrested and was taken away but the nurses, none of them were worried about them, only God knows the life stories of those who take care of, and the mountain of abuses they have inflicted upon women, children, and innocent people before their bodies were taken ill by strange diseases and weakening body conditions hence, they looking like babies needing constant attention from people like them. Furthermore; his fellow Care Home occupants were not just worried but surprised and said; so, for all these while we have been living with an old bank robber... but Jack suggested, then he is rich and if so, where is all the money stolen so for huh?

Well, this is the Meta also known as the Metaverse; the best way to get involved with it is to see it to believe, believe it to experience, and experience it to tell a tale to others. You can get on when you want and get off when you like; for the choice is yours except done something wrong with the Rules of the Meta-Quart where the Metapol comes in to address the problem. You can choose to stay, live, or quit outright but once on the Metaverse; the world of the Meta is yours to behold. The rights, the wrongs, and the privileges are up to you. Here are several societies, clubs, and other anti-social social clubs to explore without any hindrance at all. The good the bad and the ugly lie in here just that the urgency of the Metapol is seven times faster compared to that of the physical world where we all know. Hum-mm, any questions? He asked them patiently...

I don't know the exact signatures of a good society but very sure about the bad ones... here are The Freemason, The Fathers-locks, The Patriarch Roll, The Seven Steps, The Dark Book, and The Billion Dollar Grip which several Africans or the black community belongs which talks and preaches about all that money can buy, The Yamato, The Grey Frogs and Ministry of Doodoo.

Know that we are all mortals and our passions, attitudes, hobbies, professions, clubs, and political associations have brought us this far; what makes us who we are is what will make us what we can be if not checked. May we take our stand and act as such; for our destiny partly lies in our hands either you act or you would be acted upon.

They walked into the old Roman Colosseum in the Italian city of Rome and then asked what do you think happened here? Is it slavery, sports like football, or a killing spree? Disregarding what was about to happen, she branched off to the British Isle, and as soon as she got there went to the very first place the discoverer settled for his first sandwich after a long sea journey. She stepped off quite well but was a bit worried as the whole area was rough, disturbed, and angry. Miss Hello'stood on a rock that stuck out of the other seashore rocks about two meters taller and began to wonder what else matters in this place called life. She began to think, recalling all that had happened to her and what was happening and what may happen, and finally at what point she got off this hanging rock moving through space. Like an outcast thrown out from the Dutchman's ship which from history hasn't called on any port for close to one hundred and seventy years, she stood alone and thinking hard. But then, a lone seafarer in fact; a fisherman was seen puddling to the shore at a speed that is a struggle against the rough waves in the area.

So, how do you feel being alone and don't you feel left on the edge? Don't you have love once on the mainland? Hum-umm... she sounded...

This is Hagoromochalk, the most useful chalk in the world, and using it on the board takes less effort with sharp border-lines or chalk lines making the user the teacher and the student have the perfect benefit of both worlds. It has a swift and smooth speed on the board, noiseless, dustless, and no breaking in writing pace and consistency and this is what I used to teach those who worked under my attention during my sailing years as an engineer. As a tribute to the produc-ers, here is a sample I openly advertise to all whom I come across. Do you believe it or not? This is the Ferrari and even the Rolls-Royce of all writing chalks and the beauty and ingenuity of Japan, come on take this. But what gave birth to such a legend? Ahh, the best person to tell is not the creator but the good old-fashioned mathematician from the grey-haired universities, come on, go talk to them Miss... was his answer making Miss Hello to go smiling. This chalk can write, can last, and can make you feel the feelings of writ-ing... find out for yourself when you get to the city...

After the long talk over Hagoromo chalk, the long stair at it, and the millions of watts in mental mind power over the thinking of how true it is, they changed the subject and took a walk along the beach like perfect couples making plans for the unknown future. Notwithstanding that; Hello tele-trav-eled only to join the others around the old-fashioned Italian monument which has never run out of tourists in its set up as close to half a million people walk through its door per year generating millions of meta-cedi per year.

But being right, the was a warm systematic exchange of words between Miss Hannah and Miss Tracy but over what? The table of men, is it evil and can be evil? Miss Hannah was like the Table of Men popularly known as TOM is the only bad thing or ill group within the Metaverse double-crossing and mudding the affairs of the Meta Quart to every degree making sure that they make their il gain over the set-aside rules within the Metaverse and even rendering the Metapol a bit none useful Hannah challenged. And this is the truth the whole truth and may God help us all. Even listen to their slogan, to every front door there is a back door, what does this tell you huh? Say it as it is people? On the other hand; Miss Tracy began by addressing the others that; in every group or every society lies rules and regulations and rules and regulations were set by a team of experts or a leader and it's the responsibility of those leaders or leaders to make it work and that is a fact... the leaders of the Meta Quart sole responsibility is the day to day managing affair of the Metaverse and its behooves upon their mind to act and not acted upon by a third party who is and may not be a dweller of the metaverse. So; what is the point here Miss Hannah questioned sharply.

It's the weak nature or the poor supervision of the heads of the Meta Quart which has led to the rise of the Table of Men (TOM) making them do what they deem fit and even setting aside their own rules behind the backs of the cardinal rule of the Metaverse... and this is the case to be studied. And what else matters? Am even told some of the leaders within the Meta Quart are close friends and were once classmates with some leaders around the table of men, how true is that? Well, in this world, every rumor has a bit of truth behind it, and that can be the case. Mr. David Tyndallian, a British now using an American passport and living in the wide countryside of Texas, a sharp leading member of the metaverse who serves with the Table of Men said, there is an old Ghanaian proverb which says that; "Until the Lion gets their historian, the tale of the hunt will always go in favor of the hunter."

With his Oxford education and other degrees in his file, he goes to work, working for the side that pays more and not the moral value of things. As a member of TOM, he warmly and gladly postulates rules and regulations for the TOM well against the rules of the metaverse, and on every count, he is seventy percent correct; furthermore, this same man serves as one of the committee members on the council of binding rules or (COB rules) on the metaverse and has been there for close to twelve years. Margaret, a not-so-sure person in the art of conversation and mathematics from nowhere jumped into the exchange, adding that, who asked or who handpicked that old English or Anglo-American man to be part of the council of binding rules in the first place? Wasn't the person seeing or hearing the news in the air? Didn't the select committee do a background check on Mr. David Tyndallian? So, what is the point here, people, is it his fault to be on both leadership? As for me he was called and at every angle, he does his work well; hence his fat salary at the end of every month... oh, what a good businessman. What do you call this business? Making odd and ill rules to favor a select few? Is that the point here?... if so, then you are lost... Miss Hannah said and went silent.

The world which we all came from which is earth favors the bold and the willing but not the weak. Likewise; this world of Metaverse favors the Smartest and Brightest of people and not the most obedient of a kind, am I making sense? John Cool began... it is not about who or how many rules you follow or obey but what you achieve and none care about how you got it... people; it is this very act that makes things odd despite the advanced nature of the Metapol compared to the common police acts on the earth systems. I have been here drawing attention to the Meta Quart authorities over several things but so sorry to say, that some do not believe what I say and do, as such creating a teething division. At times am tired but yet not willing to give up. My name is John Cool and I have been keeping my cool but for how long?

Okay, what do you mean by saying they don't believe what you say? Jack Volt asked back... not all leaders within the Meta Quart have friends in other bodies or societies such as the Table of Men but every member who is part and parcel of the fabric of TOM has at least one close friend working within the Meta Quart or other select committee; is that okay, John began... There is a law, even set aside rules which govern the Metaverse at every stage and point but those who know the exception of that law are the friends, cronies, relatives, and club members of the very people who set up the law. That is what I have been talking about all this while, just think about it people. The laws set by the Meta Quart are just and well-formed but the exceptions are bent toward the understanding of a selected few and that is that. Hence; the law court within the Metaverse is but an Exception court whose "hearing of cases" is pregnant with conjunctions. Well, at a place where the act of believing in God is absent, I just can't say may God help us. For who is God to be considered in the affairs of the Metaverse!!

After almost fifteen minutes of silence, John Iris Rawlings went like, Ahhh-ahh what about the Youngins here? What are they learning from the big guys and how will their future be if the nature of God is not in existence here? How many churches are here and how many Mosques too can be found here?

That is a wrong question, what you must ask is whose job is it; to build a center or a place for worship and meditation here? John answered and even so, Hannah was quick to add that that is the job of the Meta Quart, am sure... it is about time to cry for Cyberwar, for peace has eluded the Metaverse, Rawlings said politely and undertone. The advanced talkative, Miss Hello has been silent for all these while and has been thinking hard only to ask openly that; so, what can we do? What can we do about what? John Cool asked her back. The ill ways of TOM and the Meta Quart which each side is turning a blind eye to some aspect of things only to fish out the weak and lone people on the metaverse to be punished and after re-educated like a Chinese Islamic faith. So, how should our behavior be on the Metaverse this time around?

Take time to school yourself and not be educated by the ill ways of others within the metaverse. Hold and withhold your ground rules on your attitude and act after a good understanding of things.

Above all; act and not be acted upon by another or even some strange event of things. Keep your location status turned on or open so; that when in danger, the Metapol may detect and come to your aid. What about the TOM? Miss Hello reminded... The Table of Men has its ways and such a well-oiled and organized group will always win, hence learn how not to be in their path or line of operation and that is a fact, people.

After John Cool had said all that; Rawlings smiled and looking at the faces of all those gathered added that; "from the rock which we were cut comes our true nature."

www.ingramcontent.com/pod-product-compliance
Lightning Source LLC
Chambersburg PA
CBHW070900160726
48004CB00003B/1172